TO SLEEP AS ANIMALS

Douglas W. Milliken

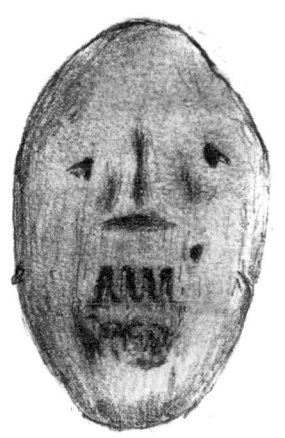

Publication Studio Hudson
Pilot Editions
2014

TO SLEEP AS ANIMALS

© Douglas W. Milliken 2014
ISBN 978-1-62462-062-1

The author would like to thank Megan Grumbling, Jacob Cholak, and Patrick Kiley for their editorial assistance, Wes Sweetser for technical feedback as well as perfecting the original glass women, Genevieve Johnson, Jenna Crowder, and Derek Kimball for design assistance, and Tanya Anderson for the invitation to Nevada in the summer of 2003.

The title page illustration is a fragment of the Igbo tribe's Osukwu ceremonial mask (on permanent display at the Museum of African Culture in Portland, Maine), as rendered by the author.

In memory of Donna Mae Bradshaw.

Publication Studio Hudson
Pilot Editions
460 Main Street
Catskill, NY 12414
www.publicationstudio.biz
pshudson@publicationstudio.biz
Printed by Patrick Kiley.

www.douglaswmilliken.com

"Adiós," she added in Spanish, "I have no house only a shadow. But whenever you are in need of a shadow, my shadow is yours."

—Malcolm Lowry, *Under the Volcano*

To
SLEEP
as
ANIMALS

Chapter 0

HE ACCEPTS THE job in the desert. He signs on the dotted line. Around him, the men lean in close to watch him write his name, and with so much bright light shining from the ceiling, no one shadow is cast. The burnt oak table shines a reflective sheen. The black floor tiles reflect a sheen. Everything, they assure him, will be taken care of. He thanks them and shakes their hands—faces like carvings in stained alabaster, their suits a flawless black: all the men, he shakes their hands—then steps out of the brick and vine building, down granite steps into clean midsummer light. Everything green and the sun swinging low. But already, above the city, storm clouds are gathering in. Weaving in darkly. Crowding out the sun. The whole scene flickers, then flickers again, and the storm light collects around him like a mantle, like a hood. He still cannot see his shadow. But that's okay. Not seeing is okay. Far off, beyond the western rains already falling, in the desert: everything is waiting. He's going back.

Chapter 1

Two weeks later at 3:30 am, gravity drags Ben Nigra from the sky to rattle him awake against the restraints zipped tight across his lap, bounce his head off the tempered porthole glass and out of his restless sleep. Outside his window stretch bright neon smears. Runway lights in a flashing grid. An opaque and watchful black. The pilot taxis to the gate and thanks them all for flying. Ben doesn't even remember having boarded the plane.

Moms with squirming children or limply sleeping children. Middle-aged men with briefcases, wristwatches, short-sleeve Oxfords. Young men with confidence setting their mouths and eyes. All of them want their carry-on bags right away. They all want back on solid ground. As they queue like cattle in the plane's central aisle, Ben makes the intentional choice to become one of them, disguises himself with the polite smile of good-natured impatience, of human beings in a line, just another tired dark-haired man in a tie.

Inside the terminal but before exiting past security, Ben stops by a flashing bank of slot machines to call his assigned escort and let him know he is here.

"Yeah, I know, I know." The voice through the cell phone is thin and irritable, like some sort of insect or broken machine. "I'm waiting down in the baggage claim right now."

Beside Ben, a silver-haired woman from his flight engages eagerly with a machine, kisses her coin and leans on the lever. The first two casters land on theatrical laughing masks. The third clicks still to a red number seven. Ben says into the receiver, "I'm almost there."

But in the baggage claim, there's no one but the other passengers from his flight, all haste and itch as they gather their luggage, retreat through the spinning mechanical doors. Shoulders bowed beneath his two carry-on bags, Ben leans against a cement column and slides to the floor in a crouch, waits for someone to approach him, a junior-academic gofer or department lackey, but while he's waiting, Ben falls asleep. Dreamless and instant and deep. When he wakes again, the terminal is empty but for a lone Hispanic janitor, wiping down the windows with a bright blue rag.

He counts slowly from zero to one hundred. Watches the janitor's wide strokes and glides. Counts from a hundred back to zero. He checks the time on his cell phone. Four-ten. Either his escort left without him or never bothered to show, had lied earlier, was not such a lackey after all. He considers calling his escort again, making him fess up and come drive Ben to his motel, buy breakfast, et cetera. He snaps shut his phone. He suspects he should feel angry. Mostly, he just feels tired. Far away, the earth is turning an expectant purple, a brightening blue sweeping through wheat fields and dusty roads, creeping like cats through eastern farmhouse windows. Far away, he is sure, the night is retreating at the threat of dawn, the scent of fresh coffee, bacon singing in cast-iron pans. He's certain, it's getting closer.

"I can do this." There's no one to hear him but the janitor, who doesn't. "I can start right now."

Dragging himself to his feet, Ben measures his stride with the scope of his breath and leads himself to the car rental desk.

THE SPACESHIP arc-sodium lamps along 395 give way to the wide-open ghost town of East Plumb Lane. Strip malls and chain restaurants closed for the night. Though he knows he should stay on Plumb for a while—past the McDonald's-and-Denny's-nowhere and into the suburbs before turning toward El's house on Pioneer—Ben can see the seductive glow of Virginia Street up ahead, the lights and the bodies that must be there swarming in the city's center. He can see the evidence and feel its draw. The darkness of these empty strip mall streets is too much like the darkness outside his red-eye flight's window, surrounding the far-flung farms of Nebraska and Minnesota, pressing down on all sides of any minor city in the night. Syracuse. Buffalo. Detroit. St. Louis. The darkness seeps like oil along the wide-open ghost town of Plumb. It's not what he came out here for.

At a stoplight, he slips out of his jacket, leaving his cell phone in the pocket. There could be cougars out there, he thinks as a dark and locked-up A&W passes on his left and again, he says it: Cougars. Dirty women and yellow-eyed men. At the next light, he takes off his tie and makes the choice, turns off his course and to the right toward the blazing neon of Virginia Street.

At the rental desk, he had asked for something efficient but durable, reliable. Something that might save him in a pinch. He was hoping for some small and anonymous thing with all-wheel drive, something Swedish or Japanese, but his lot number belonged to an '86 Jeep Cherokee, a beige Wagoneer with fake wood paneling and a definite sag to the passenger side. So it is on a dinosaur that Ben rides into town, with the blocks-long casinos projecting into the night sky on his left while on his right, cheap motels and fast food joints cluster like remoras on the sharks.

And the streets are somehow still alive. Under the false sun flashing CIRCUS CIRCUS in bubble-gum pink, the streets are wide-awake. Serious men in leather Stetsons. Blue-haired women in teams.

Marlboros and Virginia Slims. Crown Royal and coffee brandy.

And there are cougars. Dirty women and yellow-eyed men. The skeletons no one sees.

Stopped at a light outside a nightclub, Ben watches a round-hipped Asian woman in fishnet stockings and a leather skirt strutting slowly and purposefully on the sidewalk. A few yards away, near the door of the club, a tall black man in a yellow seersucker waits and watches her, is clearly bound to her. Yet when a blonde man dressed up all in denim stops to talk to her—first with quiet closeness, then with more clinging need—it's at the woman's signal that her yellow man first holds back, then in a moment, slowly draws near to loom behind her round right shoulder. When the denimed man backs away, the man and woman smile at each other, and it's clear: they like one another and like what they do. Just like the grandmothers with their buckets full of change. Like the old white men pretending to be cowboys, chewing on cigars.

This is what Ben wanted. The bodies on the sidewalks and the cars on the street. The engineered daylight pouring softly from every marquee.

Far from the door-locked shops and unpeopled avenues. Everything is safe in the light. He rolls down his window and breathes in the cool night air, leans out to feel it blow over his skin, through his hair, and at a stoplight at the corner of Virginia and Maple, Ben closes his eyes for a moment and opens them again on a different street in a darker part of town, where the lights aren't a constant gold and pink above but a flashing red and blue behind.

"No, no, I'm okay," he hears himself saying in a voice both bashful and low. "Just a little turned around is all, officer. Not even really lost."

"So you know where you're headed?" All authority, the voice pronounces from a silhouette in a wide-brimmed hat. In the gaps between Ben's words and the officer's, there is no sound at all.

"Yessir." He recites El's address, then volunteers, uselessly, "My flight just got in."

"Maybe you would like an escort." Not a question.

"No, sir, but thank you." Ben blinks at the scene through his windshield, at the tree-lined street with its parked cars and sleeping houses. He has no idea where he is. "I think I can make it from here."

Over the eastern mountains behind him, dawn slowly plows the darkness aside. But it was full dark when he was in the city. How much time has he lost again? The police officer hands back Ben's license through the open window.

"Drive safe."

"Goodnight, officer."

Ben waits until the silhouette returns to its flashing car, shuts off the strobes, pulls onto the street and drives away. He waits until the taillights shrink and disappear over a dip in the road. Through his open window: the scent of running water, and spice, and dust.

ON THE RADIO, Willie Nelson is remembering some place he might not have ever been. The lay of the light and set of the leaves. Ben snaps the radio off.

By the time he finds El's house, the sun has risen lowly above the city, shines like some white and holy thing. It's a surprise, pulling into her drive, when he finds her awake and waiting for him, sitting on her porch bench and cupping a mug of coffee in her hand, a folder of loose pages open in her lap. She remains seated for a moment as he steps out of the Jeep, sways uneasily in her dooryard. The rising sun's angled light—sky brightening behind the low roof peak—makes the whole house seem like some shadowy prop in a film about Indian burial grounds or haunted closets. It makes his head ache like a sucker punch and hangover. It makes him wonder if El is really there. But in a moment, she comes down the porch steps and meets him in the yard, arms open and pulling him in, and in the warmth of her body and clean scent of her hair, something like a brace or collar releases inside him. His spine gives up its puppet-string tension. The knot of his shoulders unties. Ben reshapes his arms to hold onto El exactly as she holds him. As if each needs the other to stand.

"Good morning, cousin."

Though of course, she's always stood easily on her own.

"You have no idea," he says into her shoulder, "how good it feels to be somewhere."

"You smell ripe," and she laughs into the ropy hair above his ear. "And you look exhausted."

He lies to make a joke about nearly falling asleep on his drive over.

"Think you can stay awake long enough to join me for some breakfast?"

Ben holds his cousin at arm's length, inspects the blues of her eyes and the red sheen in her dark hair, her sun-brown skin, the few freckles on her cheeks. The set of her mouth. The smile she can't hide. Far away, a semi downshifts and groans along I-80, then fades. The earth slows. Then it stops. A sighing breeze ruffles the untucked back of Ben's shirt, turning soaked-through sweat into a cool wet slap, and the truth is Ben doesn't think he can stay awake long enough for anything, isn't sure he's awake right now, can see this all dissolving into the smoke and haze of a dream and is almost about to say so when El smiles and wrestles his hands from her shoulders, links one arm through his and leads him to her little silver Volvo parked alongside the crooked monster of his Jeep.

"I'll take you to one of my favorites. It's worth staying awake for."

"Have you always been taller than me?"

She laughs instead of answering or maybe answers with a laugh, and as they each are about to enter her car, a police cruiser slowly drifts past down the street. The officer driving is young and wears more concern than authority in the set of his eyes, his square jaw. As he passes, the officer waves at Ben, nods in recognition. As if in slow motion, Ben is helpless but to wave back.

"Friend of yours?" Above the silver roof of her car, El's eyes are diamonds gleaming.

"Oh, yeah," and Ben swings open his door. "We go way back."

LATER BEN WILL remember his flight taking off out of Syracuse. Not the plodding wade through security, the waiting in lines or waiting in the overpriced airport taproom. Not the prolonged layover in Minneapolis where the terminals surround a central hub of expansive, unending mall. No. What he will remember is the moment his plane lifted up off the ground—the burst of speed and wet grey cityscape flashing past his window then flashing at an incline as first the front wheels and then the rear peeled away from the earth's grasp and pull—and in that one fleeting moment, the storms that had held Syracuse for weeks, for what felt to Ben like all his life, broke open and leaked out twin bands of setting sunlight to cut through the black ceiling of clouds like firelight shining through the eyes of a skull, and the city was illuminated—streets and streetlights glimmering wet with an infinite spray of shattered falling glass, prisms from the gutters and doorknobs and windows and prisms from the tips of dipping leaves—and before the darkness closed in again, sealing the city in its storm-cloud curtain, Ben escaped through the break and was gone.

AFTER THE COP left him, Ben cycled through the dawn-lit streets but failed continually to figure out where he was, how to get to where he was going, so headed straight for downtown and centered himself on Virginia Street—not by the casinos but further south, near the shops and park and the new museum for art—then headed out along the route he remembered from the last time he came to visit El years ago. Now, in El's car with El behind the wheel and the morning light full and blooming, Ben finds himself repeating his steps in reverse. Pioneer to Skyline to Arlington to Plumb, up Plumas and into town. This does not, he thinks, auger well. Repetitions and reversals in his very first hours. Does anything change your next time around? How about the time after that? Does anything change when its parts are reversed? Just joggers out now, and people trying to get to work. No red-eyed men with pockets stripped of cash. No cowboys eating cigars. Only dads hustling their children to daycare, moms trying to find parking near the office. The day-lit cogs that keep the night turning. Everyone else hides from the light.

It is while Ben works this over—this backward retracing, the city of day versus the city of night—that he briefly falls asleep again beside El in the silver warmth of her car. But when he jerks awake a moment later, it's like they're already in the middle of a conversation.

"—I mean, of course it takes up a lot of my time. And sure, most of that time is spent by myself. Or anyway, not with very many people around. But I wouldn't call it loneliness, Ben. More like…I don't know. Solitude?" And playfully, she squeezes his knee. "I'm a monk in a white jacket contemplating my navel. Only my navel's made of glass and stuck in the belly of a cow."

Ben wonders if he's awake after all.

Turning onto Sierra Street, El looks at him sidelong. "You didn't catch any of that, did you?" But she's smiling.

"Sorry, El."

Pulling up to the curb in front of a diner, its awning banded in aqua and white, El turns off the ignition and prods him with the key. "At any rate, it was kind of you to ask. So thanks." Then she adds, "Breakfast is on me, zombie boy."

Inside, the diner is a dim ghost town, almost silent, empty but for the few customers who've timed their lives around the opening and closing of these doors, regulars whose seats bear the imprint of their bodies. As if the lines of their lives have led to this place but no farther. Over coffee and hot cakes: this is where it ends. Where is there room for a stranger in such a place? El leads him to a booth along one wall. Reaching for his cell phone to check the time, Ben remembers that he left it in his jacket in the Jeep and immediately forgets why he wanted to know the time, so decides he doesn't and slides into the bench across from where El is already sitting, hands folded on her paper place mat, watching him with bemusement as if he were an animal trying to solve a simple problem.

"When did you become such a skittish little pony?"

He wipes his thumb through the dust on their table.

"The word for this place," he whispers, "is *columbarium*."

"The word for you," she says, watching him adjust in his seat, touch the napkins, touch the salt, "is *somnambulist*."

Ben bites his lip. Sleepwalking. Sleepdriving. What was he doing out there? A vibrating thread of worry begins its worming dance in his colon, but then the waitress comes over and she's tall and brown like some tropical nut and beautiful like nothing Ben has ever seen before and all at once, that anxious waver and sepulchral air are gone. She smiles before she speaks, reveals a silvery mouth full of braces. Which makes Ben love her more.

El watches Ben from the corner of her eye before finally speaking up. "We'll each have the *huevos rancheros*, over medium, and two coffees. And keep this idiot's cup full." Still speaking to the waitress, she turns her eyes on him. "I need him bushy-tailed for the interrogation."

The waitress laughs, a healthy natural sound. Ben smiles without showing his teeth and drops his head. Pushes his rolled-up napkin-and-silverware mummy around with small fingertip taps.

"She's just a kid, Ben," El says once the waitress leaves.

Ben covers his face with his hand like he's hiding. Palm over his mouth and fingers crossing his eyes. "I don't even know what you're talking about."

"Yeah, well, just try not to get arrested for sex crimes while you're here, okay? It's bad enough that you're in town on business and not exclusively to see me. I don't need you jailed too on your visit."

"They'll arrest you here for sex crimes?"

"Nevada's a strict place."

Ben thinks of the leather-skirted girls on the corner. Their watchful protectors just outside the light. The homeless men making love with their mouths to bottles inside bags.

"I see."

A moment passes in silence. A young man in red shorts and a red hat comes in with a stack of newspapers, fits them into a rack by the door, waves over his shoulder to no one in particular as he trots back out to the street. A grey-haired fellow at the counter snorts and sneezes into a dingy hanky, wipes the red bulb of his nose, snorts and stares down at his eggs, and for one fleeting second Ben sees, in the open kitchen beyond the counter, a shaggy muppet Viking monster manning the grill, glowering down at the pans. But in a blink, the monster is gone. Ben knows better than to tell El what he's seen. Overhead, the ceiling fans lazily turn.

"So," El begins, letting the completeness of the quiet come and go, "should we make-believe like we're a couple of grown adults visiting over coffee?"

"Adults?"

"Pretend like we're our parents?"

"What are those?"

Then, in an overexcited trill, "Ohmigod, it's been so *long* since I've *seen* you."

"Christ, El, no—"

"How was your flight?"

"Really? This is what we're going to do?"

"How was your flight, Ben?"

This is an old family game: being annoying.

"We go how many years without seeing one another—"

"Did you have a good flight?"

"—and you want to murder me with small talk?"

"How long have you known me, Ben? Like, forever? You think I'm going to relent? I'd give you an Indian burn or wet Willie right here and now if the mood struck. But I suspect this hurts more. Right? I'm right. I can torture you all day and it won't hurt my feelings one bit. So tell me: how was your flight?"

Against the tabletop, Ben's hands open and close like twin seething spiders, but his eyes never leave El's, and he cannot help but smile. "Goddamnit El. It was a flight. First there was synchronized sign language. Then we had peanuts.

And when there was turbulence, we all held hands and sang hallelujah and kissed our asses goodbye. I'm pretty sure I slept through the whole thing." Gazing down through the diner light sheening off the tabletop, Ben bothers the edge of his napkin. "The guy at the rental desk, though, was a real...I don't know. Full of questions, you know, and not in a way you could just ignore, either. He wanted answers. He would stop doing whatever he was doing until I answered his question."

"Like what, what was he asking?"

"Stupid things. Like what kind of name Nigra was, whether I came from a Portuguese family or something. Why I flew out here from Syracuse, what Syracuse was like, if they had a good sports franchise." The waitress stops to drop off their coffees. They each thank her and set to tearing open plastic tubs of cream. "What line of work I was in, what sort of business brought me here of all places, what series of events led me to decide to become an organ donor."

"You're an organ donor?"

"Yeah, I donate organs."

"How'd he know you're an organ donor?"

"It says so on my license. He was copying my license into his computer."

"So what'd you tell him?"

"Oh, I lied. I lied about everything."

"Why?"

"Because what's the use of truth among strangers?" But that, too, is a lie. Standing before the rental desk while the rental agent tossed his hair and held Ben's license hostage, Ben felt an acidic bubble pop in his belly each time he told the truth. "The name is Latin. As far as I know, my family's always lived in New York." After the third question, he began describing some other person, some life in another city—for a moment, became a stranger even to himself—and soon his teeth ceased to grind. It was a comfort to lie.

El probably has more questions to ask—by the set of her mouth, the way she won't stop looking at him, at his face, his mouth: definitely has more questions—but the waitress returns with their food and Ben feels himself spared. He tears into his eggs and beans with a single-minded and surprising fury. He hadn't realized he was so hungry, hadn't realized he was hungry at all. It is in this way that some primordial mechanism takes over, shouldering aside all other concerns. A lion above the fallen impala: what else is there to think about? He eats his breakfast as if it was his job and it's only once he's done that he sees how voracious he's become. And poor El, such silent dining company: she's barely halfway through her breakfast.

"Are you familiar," she asks, "with the term *pendejo*?"

"No."

"Get used to the little Mexican kids shouting it at you on the street." She takes a sip of her coffee, slowly sets down the cup. "You're going to pass out in five minutes, aren't you?"

"More like two." Sliding over, Ben leans his back against the wall and stretches his legs out across his seat. "But don't let that stop you from enjoying your breakfast. My urgency is my own. Take your time." He slowly blinks a narcotic blink. "Enjoy your *huevos*."

Which she does, leaving Ben to sip his coffee in silence, to watch the people coming in and sitting down, ordering food, talking to one another about whatever it is that people talk about, though some people don't talk at all. The too-long married, the silently too familiar. As if they've exhausted everything they could possibly say to one another. Just sit on opposite sides of a table and look at everything—the napkins, the knives, the streaks and rings left by sweating glasses—anything but one another. If these people remembered how to speak, Ben wonders, what would they say? Would they bother saying anything at all?

In the kitchen, the Viking monster does not reappear.

"One time when I was still in college," he says, "I met up with some friends of mine in Boston. None of us lived in Boston. We were all just kind of near there at a certain time, so that's where we met. These were guys I knew in high school and hadn't seen in a while, and we were all off on winter break and I think we were all seniors, so there was a certain amount of timely rowdiness in us. There might have been a point to us meeting where we met, too, but whatever point that was got lost somewhere between any number of bars. We got kicked out of almost every place we walked into. Mostly because my one friend kept harassing all the girls, saying things guys should never say in strange places to strange people, but also because we were animals. A pack of wild dogs let loose in the fusty pubs of Boston. But at the last place we went, there was another group like us, three girls who'd known each other forever and who were getting together for a drink before a Celtics game. And they liked us. Legitimately liked us. They weren't anywhere near as drunk as we were, so there's no accounting for their behavior other than an honest affection for our stupid faces and misguided attempts at charm. For about five minutes, we weren't in the wrong." Ben wipes a hand across his forehead, through his hair, lets his arm drop limply into his lap. "But you know, they had tickets to the game, so they left and then we left and that was about the end of our evening."

El doesn't look up from her eggs. "What made you think of that?"

For one second, he doesn't remember. In one silent second, it clicks back on.

"That whole night we were together, me and my friends…I don't think we said one word to one another. Maybe a few grunts and burps, but you know, no words." And he points to the various tables occupied around the room. "Just like these people here. The people who've been married forever. People who know each other too well to speak. People who maybe wished they hadn't wasted all their words all at once." He sets his hand on the table, pokes pointlessly at his coffee cup. "The way you and I aren't talking now."

She sets down her fork and meets his eyes. "The only reason we aren't talking," and she reaches across the table to put her hand on his hand, "is because you're lobotomized with jet lag."

Ben opens his mouth to make a smart-ass reply. Like it will all be okay if he can keep up with her sense of play. But when he catches her eyes, he forgets all his words, says nothing. She already knows. El smiles at the joke that neither needs to speak. Then she pinches the skin between his forefinger and thumb.

THERE ARE NINE missed calls logged on his phone when they get back to the house. It is, in fact, vibrating when he takes it out of his jacket, but he ignores that call, too. It's a Syracuse number. He has nothing to say to them yet.

Instead, he calls Dr. Snyder, his primary contact with the University of Nevada. It's only a little past eight now, but Ben figures it'd be wise to touch base with the man who helped arrange his visit here. Anyway, six of the missed calls are from Snyder himself.

"Benjamin, Jesus, I heard what happened. Joel filled me in."

"Joel filled you in." Almost a question. Joel. The no-show. The lackey. The punk.

"You'll have to forgive him, he has a humorless manner."

For no reason whatsoever, Ben pictures Snyder—has always pictured Snyder, over the course of their ten or twelve telephone conversations—as a tiny man with a colorless Van Dyke and beret, dressed completely in an unenjoyable plaid. Having never met the man, Ben has no reason for seeing any of these things. Yet the details are vivid. The image feels sharp and true.

"I can't forgive his manner, humorless or otherwise," Ben says, "because I have yet to witness it or him firsthand. I've never met the guy."

Silence from the other end. In El's driveway, Ben turns a tight circle in place, heels grinding the crushed stone. Across the street, in the open park of green grass and gangly pines, brown animal shapes distantly and indistinctly move alongside what appears to be the edge of a cliff.

"Joel says you refused a ride from him. On the basis of his posture and the color of his suit."

"Well, those sound like reasonable worries when accepting or declining rides from strange men, but I assure you: I've never met this man in my life." And after another quiet pause, "Sorry."

"No bother, moving on, let's see. We arranged a room for you at a nearby, um…. Well, we could have gotten a room for you at a location that's a bit more…comfortable, but given your stipulations, this seemed to best fit the bill."

"I'm sure it's fine."

"Mr. Nigra, if it's an issue of cost, I assure you, the University would be—"

"Money isn't a concern. It's a point of preference."

And after a brief pause: "Anyway, I'm told it has a pool, but that it's rarely filled."

"Okay."

"I hear people often sunbathe next to it regardless."

"May I have the address, please?"

Ben takes down the address and room number on the back of a matchbook that he finds tucked under the dash of the Jeep, then arranges a time and place to meet Dr. Hanover—a geochemistry researcher studying an abandoned mining settlement just south of town—early the next morning. The address and office number, too, Ben writes on the matchbook cover.

"Thanks for the help, Snyder, and hey," Ben pauses, biting his bottom lip, "don't worry about this situation with your Joel. I'm sure he's just, um"—and for lack of a more diplomatic way of putting it—"I'm sure he's just an idiot. Or something."

"He's usually quite capable."

"Aren't we all."

Closing his phone, Ben leans against the side of his Jeep, letting his thoughts skip like stones until he's not even sure what he's thinking about anymore. In the side-view mirror his eyes are heavy dark shades, the long angles of his face all pointing narcotically down. He's certain, he's not normally like this. Whatever this is.

Inside, El's house is cool and perfect and dark as a womb. From some other room, she calls out something to him, but he doesn't understand, her words indistinct in the dark. He finds the living room and finds its couch, falls pit-fallen as a stone into sleep.

WHETHER HE WANTS to admit to it or not, Ben is a dreamer, is dreaming right now on the couch in his cousin's living room. Dreams like a dog that's spent the day running through underbrush and thicket, lost or turned around, nose to the air and seeking its way home: he dreams of his day up until this moment, in flashes of color and light and smell. He dreams of the cool tiles along the baggage claim floor, the gentle hum of the conveyors droning through the concrete and the column, into his legs and spine. He dreams of people standing and sitting and standing again, strange people whose faces are vague and whose names are safely beyond his knowledge, people entering and exiting through doors that swing and doors that spin into and out of a room that is a terminal and a restaurant and an airplane and a bar and any number of other places Ben may or may not recall being. He dreams of El hugging him in the dawn light of her yard, again and again dreams of her hugging him, pulling him close, momentarily mingling his scent with her scent. Sweat and shampoo. Skin with skin. The feeling of home in her arms. Ben dreams of things he does not remember and will not remember because when he awakes, he'll forget he was dreaming at all and already, these dreams are gone.

IT'S EARLY AFTERNOON when he finally sits up from his nest on his cousin's couch. The living room is dark because this is the house's dark part. He stands and stretches, feels his mind and body renewed and liquid clear, sets out among the rooms to find his cousin.

He discovers El in the kitchen, a fan of marked-up papers spread out before her on the table. He tells her he ought to get going, will call her soon, will see her again. El convinces him to stay long enough to join her for a walk along the reservoir canal. "It'll be good to be outside and moving and breathing," she says, gathering up her papers. "Besides," and she looks from his pale face to his narrow limbs, the sag of his shirt from his shoulders, "it might do you some good to clomp around."

Outside, they cross the street and through the grassy park beneath the pines. Though the vague animal shapes here now are probably not the same shapes that Ben saw earlier, there are still vague animal shapes that, as he and El draw closer, resolve into horses ridden by young women— leather caps and tall boots—and Ben realizes: it's an equestrian park. And also true to his earlier assumptions, the park certainly ends with a cliff into a canyon, which definitely contains in its belly a trail and a reservoir canal.

"I haven't slept that much in a long time," he says, stumbling after her down the trailhead.

"You haven't slept more than five hours at a stretch?"

High overhead, a single white cloud drifts brainlessly by, the black shapes of birds gliding underneath. Ben and El start off high along the cliffs, the minor rush of water quiet and far below, but soon the trail drops steeply toward the canal. Ben was expecting to see cacti. Mostly he finds the path to be flanked by big wiry bushes and low creeping things trickling underfoot, giant thistles with bright violet blooms bursting from the rocks, and something growing somewhere nearby, under the hot July sun, smells like a chicken roasting: desert sage or rosemary or whatever native spice might abound.

A breeze picks up, cooling the sweat dripping from his brow. On the other side of the canyon, on another path, a woman in Spandex is steadily walking her dog up the grade. Above them, beyond the lip of the cliffs: the occasional swell and fade of tires on asphalt, the intermittent yell of children, the opening and closing of sliding-glass doors, reminding Ben that the private secluded feel of this place is an illusion. There are people all around. They're walking through someone's backyard.

"I'm getting the impression," Ben says when the trail slopes down and bends right around the canyon face, "that you might have taken today off on my account. Which I kind of feel bad about, having spent the majority of the day on your couch. You probably could have gotten a lot more done at the university than you could have at your kitchen table waiting for me."

"You don't need to apologize." El leans down without breaking stride to pluck a small purple flower from the brush. "You were pretty out of it earlier. You might not think so, but you were, and I could only imagine you waking up alone and bewildered and losing yourself down here." She gestures over the edge. "Trying to swim up the canal, or maybe with your leg caught in the rocks."

"I'm glad you have such confidence in me, El."

She laughs, twirls the tiny flower under her nose. "But if it makes you feel any better, I did sneak out for an hour or two. Just to make sure my lab assistant knew what to do with himself while I was out."

"Good." The path drops down sharply between twin mounds of that same dense, wiry brush, and suddenly they're walking alongside the canal as the canyon floor dips deeply within itself. Up ahead, the brush gathers close to swallow the stream while farther past, something has fallen across the water. "It's good to know I haven't obstructed your life in any way."

"Yet." And she laughs, tosses her flower into the water.

"Yet." And he watches the flower float away.

WHEN HE FINALLY leaves El's house—with El standing in the late summer brown of her lawn, waving and squinting in the sun—Ben feels himself in control. Directed and purposeful. He will check into his room. He will take stock of what he has and what he needs. He will make contact with his associates in Syracuse, if only to keep them at bay. Then he will allow himself the rare privilege of entertainment tonight.

Yet that sense of control immediately begins to slip away as the unfolding neighborhood unfolds all wrong, not at all as he had wanted. Stately street trees and houses with well-kept yards. Magisterial brick buildings with clean windows. Ben checks the address on the matchbook again, finds himself precisely where he's meant to be. Yet instead of arriving at a cheap motel, he is outside a large hall, young people pouring through the doors. He's been pursuing the wrong address. He's found the university's science center, not the motel. This is where he'll meet the geochemist in the morning.

At least I've gotten this part figured out, he tells himself as he pulls a U-turn in the street, begins again for the correct address. At least I'll be in the right place when it counts.

But then again later, he almost misses the 777 Motel: the first big gumball 7 in the sign is burnt out and dark. Pulling into the parking lot contained within the two-tiered horseshoe of the motel, Ben walks through the first door he sees but finds himself in a convenience store. Plastic-wrapped sandwiches and forties of malt liquor, microwave burritos and MD 20/20. Ben asks the clerk if this is where he should check in.

"Nah, man." The clerk is pale and scrawny and looks to be a very hard-earned fifteen. "Try the other little booth thing, over on the other side." And he jerks a thumb over his shoulder.

Back outside, Ben notes that the 777 is also the Quikie Mart #2. Booze on bottom, rooms up top.

Ben crosses to the neighboring booth, steps through the door.

"I have a room reserved," he tells the man behind the counter, an all-around healthier-looking individual with all his teeth and actual color in his skin. "It should be under Ben Nigra, but might also be under Dr. Henry Snyder, or maybe just listed with the university or some-thing, I don't know."

"A reservation, really?" The clerk laughs. "That's new."

"Yeah, uh." Ben fishes the matchbook out of his pants pocket, recites the reserved room's number, and the clerk checks a dusty black book, seems surprised to find Ben's name listed therein.

"Alright, man. Room 208 it is." The clerk slides a key across the counter. "Times must be tight if the college is putting you up here."

"It was actually by request."

"Whose request? An ex-wife?"

Ben smiles. "Something like that." Then: "Hey, would it be at all possible to have mail delivered here?"

"Man, anything is possible."

Politely, Ben smiles, makes a sound with his breath like laughter.

"What I mean is, if I use this as my address, will mail safely make it to me?"

"Yeah, we can do something like that." But the humor seems to have left this man, draining from his voice and face. "You're not going to try and make yourself permanent here or nothing, right?"

"Mine's a short stay but indefinite in length. I was told that there's a pool here."

"No man. You been lied to."

"Really? They seemed pretty positive."

But in the face of such an absurd question, the clerk doesn't even respond. Taking his key, Ben thanks the man and heads outside, gathers his belongings from the Jeep, heads up the stairs and to his room. And though it's foolish, he can't help craning his neck to look pitifully around in the hopes of finding the secret pool, that open concrete pit surround by half-naked strangers laid out on deck chairs. He suspects he needs something like it to exist. If not here, then somewhere close by.

The room is exactly what he wanted. Orange and brown décor. A colorless, worn-down shag carpet. A broken TV and a spring-shot mattress. A lovely view of some other business's parking lot.

Ben zips tight the blinds and unpacks his bags, placing everything in neat piles atop his stained bed spread.

A stack of dress clothes: two pair of navy slacks and two white shirts. A pair of olive drab Dickies and a couple white T-shirts. Regrettably, there are no shorts in his bags. A major oversight, given the 90-plus temperatures creeping steadily toward 100, but not uncorrectable. Socks, boxers, an alternate belt.

Also: several pocket-sized notebooks and two journal-sized—one orange, one black—no notes taken in any yet, as well as a handful of black, fine-point pens, one of which Ben slips into his pocket now along with a small notebook.

Breaking from his unpacking, Ben perches on the bed's edge long enough to write briefly in his two journals. In the orange one, he compares the city during the day versus the city at night, every face shaded by an intention or a need, distinct in the details but otherwise identical. In the black journal, he asks himself: *how many times will I get the details backward or the process reversed? How many times will I get it wrong?* He's certain: he's asked these questions before.

A bar of soap. A stick of deodorant, unnaturally vibrant blue. A small leather-bound album full of black-and-white and sepia-tone photographs depicting people who in all likelihood are dead or terminally old. A manila envelope stiffly packed with stacked and banded twenty-dollar bills. A slimly efficient 35mm camera. A plastic bag of film.

As he unpacks, Ben occasionally removes from his belongings a small polymer shape—wrapped in a T-shirt, tucked into a pants pocket—and sets it apart from everything else. All together, there are four of these objects, as well as a metal pin, all suggesting alignment as in a puzzle. When he's finished unpacking, Ben kneels on the floor and solves the puzzle, forming a 9mm pistol of molded carbon-fiber, bearing no name, no serial number, no marks at all but for the faint seams of the original cast. He lacks bullets, but he can find bullets anywhere. He hopes he won't have need for any.

Sitting on the corner of the bed, Ben sends a text message to the folks back in Syracuse. Tells them he's safely arrived. That he'll meet with the geochemist in the morning. The pidgin shorthand in which he types seems so ridiculous to him as to be nonsensical. He might not be sending any information at all. Just a meaningless sequence of gaps and letters. But this is wishful thinking. He knows his Syracuse receivers will understand.

His obligations for the day complete, Ben locks up his room and trots down the stairs, crosses the parking lot back to the Quikie Mart. Buys himself a hot dog and a pint wrapped up in a brown paper bag. Out on the street, grey men disguised in red eyes and dirty, incidental beards lean against the building or hunker down on the sidewalk, drinking from their paper bags with impunity. Because this is their part of town. Across the street, in front of a tattoo parlor next to another nondescript motel, women or maybe men that look like women get in and out of the cars that stop for them, come and go and come again. This is their part of town, too. Sidling in among the grey men, Ben cracks the seal of his bottle and introduces himself to the first pair of eyes he meets.

Chapter 2

THE DAY BEFORE Ben was to start the first grade, his dad set him down and explained to him the rules of proper conduct. "Always say please and thank you, even if what's offered isn't something you want. Always say ma'am and sir. If something scares you, keep it to yourself. You don't need to make people scared like you are." His dad smiled and stroked Ben's unkempt hair, ruffled it, stroked it straight. "Always keep your hands to yourself. Don't touch others. Don't let them touch you. If you have a weird thought, keep it to yourself. Don't drop your pants to your ankles when you're peeing at a urinal. Don't tell people about your dreams…."

Ben listened to the rules his dad pronounced and did his best to remember them. In later years, he'd write them on the inside covers of his notebooks. He would do his best to follow them. He would consult them as often as he needed to. He did his best to become the perfect transactor his dad wanted him to become. Even when the rules no longer applied, Ben tried to be what he thought he was meant to be.

THE NEXT MORNING, Ben wakes himself early and runs downstairs to buy a disposable razor from the Quikie Mart, showers and shaves and does his best to conform himself to the mold of public presentability. He almost doesn't recognize the man looking back at him in the mirror.

From the outside, MacKay Science Center—with its Grecian columns and mustachioed bronze statue—seems like the sort of authoritarian edifice that should maybe house an English or philosophy department. Inside, it's sterile and cool. A passing woman in a professional sort of skirt and glasses quickly spots Ben as a visitor and asks if she can help him.

"No, thank you, I'm meeting a colleague in his office."

"Are you sure? Maybe I can walk you down."

"I think I'll be okay."

Politely, the woman smiles and returns to wherever she came from. But he can tell that she's unconvinced, and moments later he too feels unconvinced when he finds the geochemist's office locked. He loiters for a while, pacing the hall, assuming that Hanover is late. He leans against the wall and slides to the floor, waits and dozes in such a way that he can still hear footfalls, in other halls, on other floors, hear voices through the walls, whispers or lectures from behind shut doors. But how long is too long to haunt a stranger's locked door? Ben heads back to where he met the smartly-dressed woman.

"It looks like maybe I do need your help after all." He finds her in a small office just off the main lobby. From the memo board and stacked file-trays surrounding her, it's clear she's the division secretary. "I was supposed to meet with Dr. Hanover in his office this morning, sometime around eight o'clock, but it appears he's not in.

Did he call in maybe to say he'd be late or was held up or something?"

The woman's smile cannot hide the obvious disappointment she feels for him. "Dr. Hanover is out at the Ophir Mill site, taking mercury samples for a study."

"Oh. So he should be back shortly?"

She shakes her head too slowly. "No. He won't be back until well after noon. He's rarely in before three o'clock." Behind her, the second hand of the wall clock methodically cuts apart the hour. "I think there must have been a misunderstanding."

"Clearly. Where did you say he was gathering samples?"

THIS TIME, HE writes his directions on an actual piece of paper, a neon green sticky-note that he affixes to his steering wheel so as not to lose or misread. Navigating through the desert plain south of the city, Ben considers calling Snyder to ream him out, to draw a clear line of comparison between the doctor and his lackey, Joel. But he recognizes the impulse as inauthentic, the thing he's supposed to want to do. Like deeming the gamblers and prostitutes somehow lesser than the city's daytime citizens. Making value judgments in the absence of value. It all mostly seems unworthy of much worry. It's easier to forget.

Drifting through the thinning suburban sprawl into the baked emptiness beyond, Ben becomes aware of the surrounding mountains. To the east—to his left—run the worn teeth of the desert foothills like the wind-whipped jawbone of a long-dead wolf while to the west rise the near peaks of the Sierra Nevadas, cool and blue-tipped and even now in summer still veined in faint snow, always veined in snow. He sees the ranging mountains as evidence of two very different worlds. And here he is in the middle. In a low spot between the two.

He forgets about calling Snyder. He turns off 395 onto Old Highway 395 and finds a country station on the radio, one that only plays classics. Patsy Cline and Johnny Cash. Hank Williams Sr. and all the other voices who don't need names to be familiar, to be known.

On their way back up the canyon along the reservoir trail, he and El cataloged the few times they'd seen each other while growing up, the fewer times they'd visited since the cement of adulthood set. "It doesn't seem right that our families lived so far apart," he said. "There's no reason why so many states should be placed between a family."

"You could change that now, you know." She nudged him playfully toward a spiky thistle crop. "I'm sure we could find some permanent use for you out here."

Ben looked up at the jigsaw ridges of the canyon, imagined a dragon's mouth slowly closing in around him. "I don't think this place would have me."

And then: "But seriously, the few visits we had growing up were really important to me. I mean, you know, I wasn't the most popular kid growing up. Always awkward and quiet and coming up with strange ideas about shadows and the spaces under trees. That's no way to make friends. Right? Most kids didn't like me. Even most adults made it obvious I was weird and wrong for being so weird. But you never cared about that at all. It didn't bother you one bit that I was so blatantly assembled wrong. It didn't matter that I was whatever I was." He laughed deprecatingly and covered his face with one hand, rubbing his eyes. "Oh, I'm getting sentimental now."

"Blame your wiring."

"Right. Faulty wiring. But I always carried that with me. You know? Like, wherever I was or whatever stupid situation I just made for myself, there was an awesome girl somewhere who loved me." Reaching the upper slope of the hill, Ben watched the horses in the park lazily plodding, their riders rising and falling with each stride, ponytails bobbing. "In that respect, I don't think much has changed for me."

El stopped him with a hand on his shoulder. "I think you're swell too, cousin." Then she pinched the hell out of his side. Now, pulling off Old Highway 395 at the stone marker signifying where the former mill once stood, Ben wonders why he bothered telling El something so obvious. Isn't the love of one's family something to reliably take for granted? Isn't that classically a constant? What had he been getting at?

Up a short drive surrounded by tall grass and twisted trees range a couple abandoned-looking buildings—one small stone structure and two larger ones of decaying clapboards and sagging timbers—and an old baby-blue Ford pickup. Several weathered post-and-board fences wind through the grass, among and around the trees and buildings, but whatever purpose or utility they're meant for seems beyond Ben's comprehension: what's to keep in or out? Stepping out of his Jeep, Ben takes a few aimless strides, turns around, squints toward the eastern horizon where the traffic on the new 395 visibly flashes through only a mile or so away beneath the ragged foothill peaks, and as Ben gazes around this place, wondering what exactly he should do now that he's here, someone audibly sniffs behind him and for the first time, he notices that a young woman is leaning against the ancient Ford's toothy grill.

"Can I help you with something, sir?" She's maybe in her mid-twenties, with a pair of blonde braids and a wholesome, Midwestern look to her face and athletic build. She's dressed in a green T-shirt and khaki shorts. In her hands is some clunky-looking electronic device. He cannot tell if it's pointed at him or not.

"Um, yeah, I was supposed to meet with Dr. Hanover this morning, but there seems to have been some sort of mix-up in locations. I was told he'd be here, though. Is that true? Is Dr. Hanover here?" Then, with a hesitancy that betrays the silliness of the question: "You're not him, are you?"

The girl smiles. "I'm guessing that gender's a weird thing where you come from, huh?"

He pictures the gangly, short-skirted figures idling outside the 777, leaning in the open windows of stopped cars.

"No weirder than anywhere else. I'm Ben." He takes a step toward her, extends his hand.

"Catherine." She steps away from the truck and takes his hand, shakes it once but firmly. Ben notices with an unusual bit of admiration the calluses on her fingers and palm. "I'm acting as Dr. Hanover's assistant today. Though hopefully not for much longer than that."

"Is that what you're doing with that?" He points to the device in her other hand. "Taking some…readings or…something?"

"Huh? Oh, no." She looks at the device in her hand as if it were something foreign and repugnant. "No, I was texting my boyfriend."

"Um."

"Yeah, that's the thing with cell phones these days. The cheaper they are, the more they look like spaceships." She slides the phone into her pocket. "Standing here sending text messages is about the total extent of my assistantship to Dr. Hanover. A very stimulating waste of my time."

"Is he nearby, maybe over—" Ben gestures vaguely toward the abandoned buildings behind him. Catherine shakes her head.

"He's taking samples from the old creek bed. There's not much of a creek left any more, but if you go through the break in the fence over there, by that tree, you'll see a little wet crease in the ground. Just follow that and you're bound to find him."

"And if I don't find him?"

"Then you'll find the highway instead."

Ben smiles but doesn't offer his hand again. "Thanks for the help, Catherine."

"Hey, anything to feel even the slightest bit useful is better than feeling nothing at all, right?"

But to this, Ben doesn't have an answer. Following the line she drew with her hand, Ben heads for the break in the fence.

THE THIN TRICKLE of creek dries up about a hundred feet east of the fence line. Ben follows the cracked-mud rut until even that seems to fade into the brown, shivering grass. He doesn't see the geochemist anywhere. He keeps walking. A little further along, under a small copse of madman-looking trees, Ben stands in the shade and the sudden wind whipping down from the mountains, lets the wind have its way with his clothes and with his hair. He considers leaning in the shadows under a tree and closing his eyes, letting the time slip by until he has something to do, but eventually a husky figure wearing what looks like a fishing vest comes tromping out of the grass and into the shaded copse.

"I imagine you're Mr. Nigra." Beneath the shading brim of his sun hat, the man is bearded and squint-eyed. He speaks with the faintest hint of a British accent. Ben immediately determines: it's an affectation. "I was wondering when you'd show up. If you'd show at all."

"Believe it or not, I was on time." Ben lets a deliberate moment pass before offering his hand. "I was told you'd be at your office."

Hanover looks at Ben's extended hand but makes no effort to take it. "That's a pretty stupid thing to have been told, Mr. Nigra. It is Mister, right?"

"Right."

"Not doctor."

"Right."

Hanover smiles humorlessly. "You'll have to forgive me, but being a scientist, a man of exacting and exact knowledge, I have to ask: is it *Nye*-gra or *Nee*-gra?"

"The first one."

"I suppose it doesn't matter, really," and the geochemist laughs. "The meaning's the same no matter how you say it."

And now it's Ben's turn to smile without humor. "In a particular instance, Nigra can actually mean 'Austrian,' but as fascinating as my name might be, I'm actually here to learn more about what you do."

This dialogue, he notes, is not starting off well.

"If you'd been here an hour or so ago, I could have shown you firsthand. As it is, you'll have to settle for a summary. Come along." Like a schoolmarm or minister, Hanover walks away with his hands clasped behind his back, his strides long and purposeful. Half-tempted to call the whole meeting off, to begin a new line of inquiry, Ben silently follows.

As they get closer to the highway, the grasses thin out to hardpan and large stones and more of that same wiry brush that flourished throughout the reservoir canyon. Far ahead alongside the highway, some sort of dome or quonset facility stands amid a crown of fishhook street lamps and somewhere in between, among the grasses and the brush: cows, grazing.

Keeping a purposeful distance ahead, the geochemist explains the various histories of this site in an intentional, opaque jargon that Ben understands is meant to confuse him, make him feel inferior. Most of this, he simply ignores, choosing instead to watch the brush shiver in the breeze, scrutinizing the spaces between stones for darting rabbits or fox or quail, waiting for the geochemist to talk himself out. Eventually, Hanover explains the settlement of the area. How gold and silver ore extracted from the Comstock Lode were reduced to pure metals at this and other mill sites in the region. How mercury was a major component in the reduction process. How none of the various techniques were terribly efficient. "Ridiculous amounts of gold and silver were washed away in the creek. And, of course, plenty of mercury, too." The creek, Hanover assures him, was once much more than it is now.

On the highway, the driver of a Mack truck pulls the cable for his horn and keeps it pulled as it roars by, its ongoing blat trumpeting down and fading as it goes. The geochemist stops in his tracks to watch the truck go by, something like boyhood hurt or wonder filling his thick, squinting eyes. Ben studies the man, waiting. In a moment, Hanover tromps on through the grass.

Some ten years ago, the geochemist continues, a study had been conducted—here and at the other abandoned mills—to determine the sources of the unusually-high levels of mercury found in Washoe Lake and other waterways in the county—"Which is to say, Mr. Nigra, mercury found in all the drinking water in the region"—

wherein it was concluded that, in conjunction with the overall rise of industry, residual mercury from over a hundred years ago was still leaching into the groundwater.

"So what are you doing out here now?" Above them, the sun stares down merciless and unblinking, boiling the sweat from his skin, but somehow Ben doesn't seem to mind. He almost likes the heat. "If your predecessors figured this out already, why are you still taking samples?"

"Because, Mr. Nigra, mercury levels have been rising. One would expect them to diminish over time."

"And you think somehow more is leaching from this site than before?"

"It is possible. Seismic activity could release large, previously dormant caches, for example."

"But you don't think that's the case." Ben stops, waits for Hanover to do the same. "Do you?" But the geochemist keeps walking, weaving his way between the stones, and Ben suddenly realizes that Hanover isn't leading him anywhere, is simply wandering through a grassy expanse while the roar of the highway grows closer and closer.

It occurs to Ben that this man is a useless cog in an outdated academic machine. Making work for himself by reopening closed cases. Chasing dead ends. Doing nothing and getting paid.

"Why are you out here, Mr. Nigra?" Hanover takes off his sun-hat, mops the sunburnt dome of his bald scalp with a handkerchief. "This isn't your professional interest. This isn't even tangentially related to what you do back wherever it is you come from. So why are you here?"

"Why did the mill close down?"

"What?"

"The Ophir Mill. Why'd it close down?" Up ahead. Hanover finally stops, slowly turns in his tracks while Ben continues to speak. "People worked here and lived here and now they're all gone. Was it because they'd poisoned their water with mercury?"

"At that time, they didn't know it was poison."

Something between disgust and amazement seems to be shaping the geochemist's face, but from so far away, Ben can't be sure.

"So then what happened that made everyone pack up and leave?"

"Wh—what *happened?* The twentieth century happened. Are you for real, sir?" Hanover retraces his steps, brings himself within easy arm's reach of Ben. "The American West is full of places that no longer serve a purpose so have been left behind. It's how this country copes with old age."

"And that," Ben says, "is exactly why I'm here."

"I do not follow you, sir."

"Don't you think the people here fought to keep what they had?"

"If they really wanted it so bad, Mr. Nigra, they'd still have it." The crease in his brow is a fissure down a mountain face, his mouth's smug set dissolving. "What are you after, Mr. Nigra? You come out here with the university's compliance and aid to pester me with questions more appropriate to a historian or a—a *librarian.* A fifth-grade schoolteacher would be a better interviewee than I would. Yet here you are tramping through my lab and wasting my time with this foolishness. So why are you here? Why are you bothering me with these questions?"

Then: "What are you trying to drag me into, Mr. Nigra?"

Ben casts his face into the shape of long-suffering patience and waits for this tantrum to play itself out, but with a sudden flicker—like a series of frames badly edited from a film—he feels as though some time has passed. Both men stand just as they had a moment before, but somehow the light is different, a cloud is moving across the sun and Hanover is demanding that Ben repeat what he just said, asking why he'd say such a thing, though as far as Ben can recall, he hasn't spoken a word.

Finally, his temper exhausted, the geochemist says, "I think you might have gotten your Ophir Mills mixed up, sir. There's another one, about a hundred miles east of here. If it's ghost towns you're after, Mr. Nigra, that's the one you want. Lots of ruins and mysterious intrigue. Now I'm done being polite here. I'm done talking to you altogether." Hanover turns and heads back into the rocky plain, purposeful and quick in his stride. Ben watches him go, then turns back the way he came.

Over the sound of the highway, over his shoulder, Ben thinks he hears once more, "If it's ghost towns you're after..." but the rest is lost in the wind or was maybe never said.

On his way back, just past the shadowed grove where Hanover earlier found him, Ben stops at a low stone structure he hadn't noticed before. Tucked in alongside the dried-up creek, under the boughs of a snake-nest tree. He peers through the windows but cannot see past the dim rime of dust. A heavy metal padlock looped through a hasp riveted into the door: of course, it's locked.

Ben looks into the far off grasses where Hanover cannot be seen. He looks toward Old Highway 395, where Catherine can't care less what he does. Searching the creek bed, Ben comes back with a rock, rounded on one end and toothed on the other, and pounds the lock off the door.

A dirty floor. A dusk of floating dust. A crumpled newspaper jammed into a corner. Not even an old paper, either: no period documentation of mill life, on the depletion or boon of ore from Comstock or Silver City. Just some local news from two years ago bragging at the city's proud reduction of gang violence during the previous three Hot August Nights.

What's the point of protecting this, he wonders. Why keep this empty space so precious and preserved? Yet the sheer fact of this place—of locking up and maintaining a place so obviously abandoned—is a sort of evidence in and of itself. It's precious because it's abandoned. Before he leaves, Ben snaps a few pictures—the crumpled paper, the dust caught in the light—then pulls the door closed as if he was never there.

"Your boss is a real asshole."

Catherine looks up from her rocket-ship cell phone. As far as Ben can tell, she hasn't moved since he left.

"Yeah, but in a few hours it'll be over and I can move on with my life. I think I can survive the wait."

"What, are you quitting or something?" Ben stops a few yards from her and takes off his jacket. His head is light and vaporous. He's sweated through his shirt.

"No, it's a temporary assignment. No one can work with Hanover for more than a few days before seriously reevaluating their doctoral ambitions." There's something in her cadence that rings false to Ben's ears. "As a means of communal self-preservation, all the post-grads in the science program take turns babysitting." Like she's trying to sound smarter. Catherine reaches behind her neck to adjust the lay of the braids across her back. "It's the sort of policy that is officially recognized as not being a policy, if you know what I mean."

"So this"—and he gestures vaguely over his shoulder, taking in the slouching buildings, the shaking grass and trees, the far-off highway and, in the midst of it all, the red-faced geochemist—"all this work with Hanover, this isn't necessarily your field, is it?"

"Mercury studies bear about as much personal pertinence," she says, "as French naval strategy during the Crimean War."

Ben pauses a beat: "So no, you don't study geochemistry," and he's glad she laughs, if even nervously.

"Sorry. I'm used to competing with my classmates. Everyone always trying to sound smart, even if what they're saying is vapid or dull."

"I think we're all guilty of that." Awkwardly, he moves his jacket between his hands. He's not sure what to do with it now that he's taken it off. "So what *is* your field of study?"

And right then, something in the way Catherine looks at him seems familiar. As if she were trying to figure out something about him that he didn't know needed figuring. It's the same look Hanover gave him among the rocks and dead grass. "It's kind of hard to explain." It's a look he's seen repeated endlessly throughout his life. "But essentially I'm studying the symbiotic behavior of certain plants, fungi, and bacteria."

"What sort of symbiosis?"

She pauses before she speaks. "Um, there are a few that I'm studying. But mostly I've been working with *Sarcodes sanguinea*, also known as the Tahoe Indian pipe or the snow plant. They're little red mushroom-looking things that spike up out of the ground, but their roots are completely wrapped up in a coat of fungi that provide almost all the nutrients and water the plant needs to survive."

"How do they do that?"

Again, that pause. As if wondering how she should answer or if she should answer at all. "I think the best way to understand it is like drinking water through a straw. The roots of the Indian pipe are so thoroughly covered in the fungi that they have virtually no direct contact with the soil. The fungi is the plant's conduit to everything it needs."

"Why do they do that?"

"Excuse me?"

"It seems like such irrational behavior. I mean, the Indian pipe or whatever it is, it gains a pretty obvious benefit from the fungi, would probably die, I imagine, without it. But what's the fungi have to gain?"

"Well, that's sort of what I'm trying to find out in my research."

"So you're looking to prove a symbiosis where one does not necessarily exist?"

"Why are you so interested in this all at once?"

Something is changing in the air between them. Ben worries it might have already changed. "Why shouldn't I be?"

"I thought you came here to learn more about Dr. Hanover's mercury obsession. Now you're acting like I'm part of your...investigation or whatever."

"It's not an investigation. Are there any of these Indian pipes around here? I'd like to see one."

"No."

"Could you show me where some might be?"

"I don't think that's a good idea." It suddenly occurs to Ben that she's frightened. Her eyes are wide and she's backed up against the pickup's grill and it's him that she's afraid of. As if he's trying to trick something away from her. Nodding, Ben puts his jacket back on—"Fair enough, thank you for your time"—walks back to his still-ticking Jeep. But before he can get in, she calls for him to stop.

"The Indian pipes are mostly up around Lake Tahoe. I'll call you before I head up next time." She brushes an errant strand of hair from her eyes, tucks it behind her ear, and though she's trying to remain composed, he can see: the hand in her hair is shaking. "Maybe I could show you one then."

Ben thanks her, recites his number, watches her type it into her phone. He tries to smile, harmless and avuncular. He's not sure she's convinced. Pulling out of the mill's long driveway and pointing his Jeep north, Ben chews his lips, stares vacantly at the road. Sees her shaking hand in her hair. Hears the break again in her voice, promising that she'll call.

On his way back from the mill, Ben stops at the quonset facility he saw while following Hanover through the aimless fields. He pulls off at the open gate but does not drive through it, does not get out of his Jeep. Tall arc-sodiums fishhooking up from the parking lot surrounding a cinderblock and steel hump rising from the desert buff and stone. Like the mouth of a passage leading into the earth's belly. Like some secret he isn't supposed to see. Cyclone fence and razor wire. A sign bolted to the open gate explains this site via an indecipherable acronym, but in yellow and black compound triangles above the blast door, another sign explains in much clearer, more terminal terms:

FALLOUT SHELTER

Ben tries to take a picture but before he can, a man in a grey jumpsuit appears out of nowhere, asking who he is, why he's here, and without answering, Ben guns the engine, drives away.

BECAUSE IT'S BEEN on his mind since he passed it outside the airport—because, whether he likes it or not, his body sometimes calls the shots—Ben drives to the A&W on Plumb. Its sign a branding iron held high into the air. Its parking lot redolent with the scent of seared meat. But as much as he'd like to go inside—the polished glass doors, the paper hats behind the register, the orange and brown and cream white everything, the rubbery kiss of the bench seat booths—Ben imagines the traffic of bodies sweaty and hungry queuing in a constant flow in and out of those same glass doors, their needs and conduct so obviously barnyard, and he cannot go inside. He steers through the drive-thru, orders a burger, fries, an enormous root beer, and even when passing the cash through the window or when being handed his bag of food, he does not have to look inside, does not see the person on the other side of the glass. Neither eyes nor hands touch during the transaction.

What a comfort, he thinks, to be anonymous and not mean anything to anyone. How nice to pass like a ghost.

Though it seems like a tactless move to make in the company of a greasy lunch for one, Ben swings by his cousin's house to see if she might be around, but he doesn't even need to stop to know she isn't home. At the end of her street, he turns left off Pioneer onto Skyline, cruises past a firehouse and another canyon-side park—adjacent to the equestrian park, with ball fields and playground equipment, slides and swings—the street steadily climbing to the top of the hill, and where Skyline meets McCarran and ends, he pulls an awkward U-turn and drifts back down Skyline. Pulls over and parks near the playground. Eats his lunch while watching the children run and scream.

His phone rings twice while he eats. Snyder. He ignores the calls, eats his burger, throws fries out his window for passing birds he hopes will come but do not, finally dumps his soda out the window and throws the empty cup on the passenger side floor, starts the engine and goes. The radio tells of how a rape victim overcame her attacker by gouging out his eyes. That, Ben thinks, is a fucking smart move. Drifting along the residential edges of town, he soon finds himself winding through a burgeoning development—new roads and half-built homes—and when the phone in his pocket again begins to buzz, he pulls off alongside an excavated lot furnished only with a cellar hole and dumpster.

"Afternoon, Doctor."

"Benjamin, I'm so glad to finally reach you."

Snyder's voice is a smoky rasp, slightly slurred. Likely a pipe clenched tight between his teeth.

"I have to admit feeling somewhat sheepish, Dr. Nigra. It seems I'm always apologizing these days for one associate of mine or another."

"Mr. Nigra."

"Excuse me?"

"There's no need to apologize," Ben says. Out from behind the dumpster, a yellow dog jerkily trots, tongue lolling and eyes wide. It stops when it sees his idling Jeep but seems neither curious nor afraid. "Least of all for your associates."

"Despite the impression you might have gotten," Snyder goes on, "Dr. Hanover *was* supposed to meet you at the Science Center this morning. At least, after having spoken to him last week about your interest in the abandoned mill site and the likelihood of your interview, he indicated *to me* that he would meet you at his office. Perhaps I misunderstood, but—"

"Wait, did Hanover talk to you already?" Outside, the dog drops down into the dust. "Did he contact you after our meeting? Or did you get a hold of him?"

"Well, neither." On its back, the dog rolls and writhes, kicking up a small cloud of dust. "I spoke with the division secretary and she explained what happened."

"You asked her directly about my visit."

"Yes."

"Asked her how it went."

"Yes, precisely, and was dismayed to learn not only about his absence but also about his lack of cooperation once you found him down in Ophir Mill."

"Hanover told the secretary that he did not cooperate with me?"

"Hanover's assistant told her. The secretary called his assistant to follow-up on things, make sure you made it to the mill site okay. Honestly, Benjamin, I'm aghast at Dr. Hanover's lack of tact and to be perfectly frank…."

Watching the dog playing in the dirt while Snyder's voice drones on in his ear, it occurs to Ben that—given his arrangement with the university, the contacts he's asked for and the access he's been granted—Snyder is trying to keep tabs on him.

He thinks of the miscommunications and the failed rendezvous. Thinks of Hanover's assumption as to the purpose of Ben's project. Of Catherine's apparent knowledge of him, and her fear. As if everyone in the university already knew his name and had made up their minds as to who he was before he'd even stepped off the plane. Like the deck was stacked from the start.

"—that said, I guess if I'd know that it was the fact of the settlement's *abandonment* that most intrigued you, then—"

"That's not entirely it, sir."

"Well, regardless. As a measure of recompense, I've arranged for another of the department's—"

"You'll have to excuse me, Dr. Snyder," Ben interrupts as outside, half self-interred, the dog gives a tiny yelp, "and please do not consider this a lack of appreciation for what you've done and how much you've helped, but I think at this juncture my project and I might fare better on a more solitary track."

Silence. Near the cellar hole, the dog kicks its legs in the air, wriggles and moans low in its throat. After a few preliminary sounds of protest, Snyder accepts the new condition. "Very well, sir. Understand that per our original agreement, your access to the university remains unfettered."

"Thank you, it's definitely appreciated. And necessary, I'm sure."

"Please let me know if there's anything more I can do to help."

"Will do."

The connection snaps closed with a click. Dropping the transmission back into drive, Ben pulls off the shoulder, turns around at the cul-de-sac's end. As he passes the bare lot on his way out, the dog runs out into the road to follow along beside the Jeep, and it's only then that Ben sees its fur is patchy with mange, the skin beneath enflamed angry red and visibly swarmed, pustules broken, so riddled with fleas that they've burrowed under its hide. What he thought was a game was a vain attempt to peel away its skin. And as the dog runs alongside the Jeep to gaze up into his open window, Ben can clearly see what this animal wants, what it's begging for, and he wishes he could somehow comply. Even as he pushes the accelerator and speeds away. Even as he leaves it behind.

BACK IN THE CITY, Ben parks on a side street near his motel and starts off on foot, weaving among the major and minor thoroughfares and alleys surrounding the 777. Last night, while enjoying his pint in the company of other lost wanderers,

Ben learned from several of the grey men that the only way to survive on one's own on these streets is to make one's mind into a map. "You've got to know in an instant," explained Earl, a former bank administrator from Indianapolis with an electric shock of dirty hair and half his left ear missing, "where you can run or hide, if there's a gate you can lock, whether this or that fence you can crawl under or go over. If there's a window you can sneak though, you know. Anything." Ben offered the man his bottle. Earl drank lovingly without touching his mouth to its lip. "Sometimes the kids here are like wild dogs," and he handed back the paper bag. "Sometimes the cops're even worse."

So Ben turns his mind into a map, braids his synapses into the gridded topography of his new adopted neighborhood. The steel drainage grate leading under the street, bolts missing and one corner popped out like a poorly-thread lid. Alleyways between cantinas and taquerías, dumpsters and stray cats and rats. The windowless burnt-out hull of a house festooned in yellow tape. A small shed with a broken lock almost invisibly tucked behind the corner of an imports record store.

Whether I use these places or not, Ben thinks, it does me no harm to know they exist. There are happy homes and clean kitchens and no secrets kept behind familiar kissing lips. But there's also this.

It's almost inevitable that, among all this, Ben finds—Confederate flag over the door and deer heads hanging in the window—Bill's Rifle and Reload Center. It's inevitable what he finds inside.

Chapter 3

When Ben was a boy, he once clearly saw the shape of the sun passing behind a thin scrim of clouds. He had climbed a tall oak tree overlooking a creek that ran through the vines and brush behind his parents' house, had slithered out to perch on a sturdy branch above the water. Legs dangling far above the ripple and purl, he had contemplated the ideas of up-ness and down-ness until it became obvious to his eight-year old mind that neither concept existed, that neither up nor down could be achieved in the context of trees or rivers or the invisible hand of gravity. And as he sat frozen by his own discovery on this summer-lit branch—unable to climb further up or retreat down—the sun slipped behind a cloud and Ben saw clearly the shape of the sun. Perfectly round like a penny glowing beneath a torch's flame. The volatile and burning heart and mother of the solar system. Completely superceded by a vaporous mask of water and dust.

With impunity he watched what had once been mighty be demoted to a mere hot coin in the sky. But when the clouds moved aside, the sun's light blinded Ben in a flash and he closed his eyes, hid his face in the shoulder of his shirt, and with all bets off as to certainty and absurdity, Ben revised his recent paralyzing theory. The clouds circled the earth and the earth circled the sun and the sun circled something greater and gravity cinched all the lines taut. There was no up-ness, only down-ness. He slid off the branch and into the river below.

FOR THREE DAYS, Ben wanders the city's tangled matrix of streets. He haunts the downtown library—with its lush tropical plants and draconian rules that seem designed less to protect the archives and more to prevent anyone from finding anything ever—then the Cubist sculpture of a library on the edge of town, then finally the university's campus library. He tries to pick up threads, talk to people, get involved in something. Mostly he drifts among the stacks, stupefied by the magnitude of titles and the corresponding lives wrapped up in filling the space between covers with words and, presumably, meanings. All these people searching and finding and reporting what they found. By turns, he feels worshipful at the enormity of their collective effort, perplexed by the futility, dumbfounded by the result.

He looks up a lot of pictures of the Tahoe Indian pipe at the severe downtown library, using a computer and an online database affiliated with the Library of Congress. In some pictures, the snow plant appears as a venereal Martian creature, unfolding one obscenely red petal at a time. In others, it looks like a battered penis. But the librarians forbid him from making any copies of what he finds. So he leaves empty-handed. Despite the lingering images in his memory, it feels like he's found nothing at all.

Sometimes he transfers notes from his pocket notebooks to his orange journal or black journal, expanding and rearticulating the things that he's observed. The relationships between various bodies on huge and miniscule scales. The reasons things come together, fall apart. He does his best to make things cohere.

At night, he wanders the casino floors, parking in front of a slot machine long enough to be noticed by a waitress, score a free drink, move on. He follows the Truckee River as it meanders through town, walking its banks into unlit dead zones until he no longer feels safe, walks a little farther with its wet whisper singing in his ears, keeping him company in the dark.

He calls his friend in Boca, just over the stateline into California. He'd almost forgotten: he has a friend in Boca. A glass artist. Calls him two or three times. But no one ever answers. Each time, a machine records him mutter and hang-up. Yet he continues calling his friend in Boca. Someday, someone has to answer.

At the end of the third day, Ben invites El to join him on his search for the other Ophir Mill, the one that Hanover had mentioned. He knows it's a silly chase, following the backhanded suggestion of a dumpy false Englishman. But tomorrow is Saturday and he's lonely and lost in his own futility, and because she does not need to be at work that day, El takes him up on his offer. "It'd be good for us both, I think," she tells him, "to get out of town for a while." Ben stands with the phone, peeking between the slats of his blinds at the parking lot below where two Mexican boys share a bicycle, rolling around in circles, one perched on the handlebars, laughing, rolling around and around. He tells her he'll pick her up tomorrow at dawn.

THE ROOMS ON EITHER side of Ben's fill up and empty and fill again. Moans and screams and laughter and panic. One woman begs to be untied, but in the way she says it—hot fast pants and snarling noises—Ben doesn't think she should be believed.

IT'S DARK WHEN HE awakes sitting up in a chair beside the window, his album of black and white pictures open in his lap. Dark when he peels out of yesterday's clothes to shower. Dark when he dresses in the clothes he just took off. Like a deep purple cloth has been pulled over the sky, fetched up and draped over the peaks of every casino and hotel along Virginia Street, swallowing whole the little houses in the valley. A bright blue vein edges the eastern mountain-line. He doesn't remember having fallen asleep.

Outside, near his Jeep, Ben finds some grey men gathered, smiling and eager to see him. As if they'd been waiting through the night.

"Ben, Ben," Earl says, the mouthpiece for the others, stepping forward when the others hang back, "we missed you last night, my man."

"I stayed in."

In a one-sentence letter delivered to the front desk: the folks in Syracuse had recommended he stay in.

"We found something last night." Earl is grinning. Like an excited child or an idiot, Ben can't tell which. "Something we'd like to show you. Something we'd like to share."

"Thanks, Earl." Ben smiles, smiles over Earl's shoulder to the other men and waves. "Thank you." They wave back. "Maybe tonight you can show me. I have to be somewhere right now, but maybe tonight or tomorrow."

"What, you think maybe you got a date or something?" And the way Earl leers, now suddenly neither a child nor an idiot. More like something ghostly and mean disapparating through the morning's thin breaking.

"I've got a cousin is what I've got."

"What you got is trouble," and in the dim non-light before dawn, with every other streetlight flicking on, flicking off—in an inverse Cheshire cat solution, Earl's grinning mouth disappears while the rest of him remains.

By the time Ben gets to El's—after detaching himself from the grey men, after weaving like a needled thread through the transitional streets of just-waking or nearly-sleeping, heavy-eyed bodies—the sun's crept up enough to show the sky to be a rippling fish belly of clouds floating bluely toward the mountains. From her waiting porch, El jogs—nearly bounces—down the steps and through the yard into Ben's Jeep with a backpack and a thermos full of coffee. They say good morning with yawning good cheer and head out east along I-80, rushing to meet the sun.

El pours him coffee, turns on the radio and changes the station. First Nirvana comes on. Then Weezer. They sing along, each laughing at how terribly the other sings. Somewhere near Fernley, Ben realizes this is their first roadtrip together.

He also realizes the geochemist's estimate of a hundred miles is way under the mark. Glancing at a map while waiting in line at a gas station outside Fallon, Ben measures the distance with thumb and forefinger, checks the scale, and more than doubles the distance. Without seeming in a rush, he keeps the needle between 90 and 100 after that. But with nothing but empty desert on either side of him, it barely feels like they're moving at all. Like the background scenery in an old cartoon, passing swiftly but quickly repeating, leading to the overwhelming conclusion that running and standing still result in the same exact thing. El pours him more coffee and watches the desert repeat outside her window. In the rearview mirror, Ben watches the rising spume of dust feather up behind the Wagoneer. For a long time, it's all he watches. It's his only evidence that they're actually in motion. After a long stretch of miles, silent though not uncomfortable, Ben remembers his manners and finally decides to speak.

"El?"

"Yes."

"What's Hot August Nights?"

"It's a car show."

Along the highway shoulder, a coyote casually trots, head high with a rabbit hanging from its jaw.

"Gangs get violent at car shows out here?"

Just as they pass: off into the sagebrush it drops.

"We're a passionate people."

WHEN BEN HIT THE water and first sank until his sneakers touched the creek bed's gravel and muck, then rose to float between the surface and bottom, the eight years that made up his life seemed impossibly long. In the context of rivers and trees and the snagging grasp of gravity's hand, how could life seem like anything but an endless warp and weave?

Floating downstream, watching the creek bed unfurl like a flag beneath him, the intricate web of his own existence—the sequences of learning to count then add, subtract then multiply, the chain connecting himself to his parents to his aunts to his cousins, of his own limbs manifesting from the tadpole he already understood himself to have once been—every detail that completed the puzzle of his life seemed massively important and beautiful, but as he turns off US-50 and onto 376, trading one vacant stretch of Nevada highway for another, Ben feels anything but wonder-struck awe for the unending circuitry of his life. Less like a limitless matrix and more like a Mobius strip, some sort of purgatory.

From her backpack, El produces a peanut butter sandwich and tears it in two, gives him the greater portion.

"This road," he says, "stretches forward and stretches back. But I'm always in the middle."

"You should be on the right." But even through her joke, he can sense an edge of worry. Toward his face, she pushes the sandwich in his hand. "Eat."

He watches the wind move snakes of dust across the crackled pavement. Side-winding and then gone. He does what she tells him to do.

THE ROAD DOWN IS a ragged dirt scratch skittering off the edge of 376, wriggling among dust and rocks to eventually climb up along the ridge of a small foothill peak, then drop back down into a minor canyon. Sometimes the road seems more of a suggestion than an empirical truth. It makes Ben glad to have the Jeep.

Beside him, each time they hit a rut or bump, El bounces and laughs, rebounds off the door, against his shoulder, rattles around like a bolt in a bucket.

"Whoa.

"Oh."

More laughter.

"Oh God."

When it seems foolish to push the rusted-out Wagoneer any further up the trail, he kills the engine and they set out on foot. But it's not far.

Ben can see the edge of a stone-built something peeking from above the next ridge.

"I feel like I'm walking through the apocalypse," El says as they cross over the crest overlooking the ruins below. "Or anyway, like the set to a movie about it."

Ben pictures the twisted doomsday trees along the desert highway and around the other Ophir. He pictures the grey streets of Syracuse or Buffalo or Erie in January, trash bags rattling and discarded Christmas trees half-buried in curbside slush. Pictures the outer darkness swallowing every minor ranch and township beyond his airplane window. "I've seen worse."

For a while, they walk along together, inspecting the ruins as a team. El keeps picking things up, turning them over in her hands, sometimes rubbing a spot clean with her thumb and a drop of spit. Her excitement just another tool for discovery. Ben wishes he could feel that way. He wishes her excitement were contagious. But soon enough, they split up. While El investigates a flat expanse near a cracked and collapsing wooden fence, Ben hikes up the crumbling rock face, in among the partial structures and heaps of time-knocked cobbles. A lone stone wall two stories tall with empty windows gazing westward. A roof and three walls housing the fallen remains of the fourth. A rusty length of an unidentifiable tool. A spray of broken green glass.

From a rock high above, Ben looks down to watch El carefully step among the stones, holding the loose strands of her hair under her chin like bonnet strings, occasionally ducking down to inspect something or other amid the limitless scree.

She looks like a little girl, he thinks, watching her. This is what she was like as a girl. But when he tries to test this claim against the evidence of his memory, he comes up empty. He cannot picture her as a child. In all his memories, she looks as she looks now. As if he's replaced what was with what is. As if he always has.

Down below, El stands up quickly, raises something up in her right hand into the air. "Look!" She's still holding her hair like bonnet strings to her chin. He has no idea what she's found but pretends he does, laughs appreciably, runs down the slope to join her.

THEY EAT THE LUNCH El packed in the half-moon hollow at the base of a stone silo, eat cold roasted pork and hunks of sweet potato wrapped in corn tortillas in the cool dark shade. For the most part, neither speaks. In a mutual, comfortable silence they chew, drink the last of the coffee, watch the long unchanging plain continue to go unchanged. Outcroppings of stone. The occasional crippled bush or tree. The far-off empty gouge of 376. The open sky and hot lashes of sun.

Afterward, they spread out again, stake out a wider perimeter, slowly scanning the stones ahead and stones underfoot. El keeps to the flatland at the bottom of the shallow canyon's stone shoulder. Ben keeps to higher ground, careful of his footing yet still, now and then, sliding down.

He finds a slim structure built into the side of the rock face, but inside—by the light of gun-slot windows and the light of a couple matches—Ben finds nothing but a cable spool set up as a table and a mat of bunched-up burlap rotting in the corner. He finds a square of wrought-iron fence surrounding a four-by-four plot of the same undifferentiated desert stretching outside the metal square. He climbs the solitary two-story wall and positions himself in a window, looks out at the plains below, but it's hard for him to focus on the landscape. As if everything distinct disappears under his scrutiny, dissolves in a wash, and is gone.

After a while, Ben loses track of El, so sets off to find her, heading farther west and away from the Jeep, deeper into unexplored territory. He finds more ruins and an old open well, but when he hollers down, no one but his echo responds. He finds a shovel so rusted through that it falls to splinters and dust in his hands. But he doesn't find El. Out this way, there is no trace she's ever come.

Walking back, Ben sees high up on the rock face two tall narrow slots carved into the stone, on equal footing and spaced maybe twenty feet apart. Like a Halloween death mask carved into the canyon's face. Two blind eyes in the vacant face of some forgotten thing.

Ben thinks about the geochemist's residual poisons still leaching after a hundred years. He thinks about the coating fungus clinging to a red pipe's milky roots. Ben climbs the slope up and into the first gap in the bank.

Though it's dark inside, enough light streams through the opening and past Ben's shoulders to illuminate the narrow passage, carving straight into the rock and bending sharply to the right ten or twelve feet in. Pebbles and tiny bits of metal junk litter underfoot. Ben has to turn sideways to crab-step through.

Around the bend, Ben stops and stares. An indeterminate distance in, the passage bends again to the right, becomes the other opening in the rock face: he can see the daylight pouring in to pool in the elbow's crook. But between here and there—from one thin splash of light to another—there's only darkness. Boundless and pure.

Reaching out, Ben feels the walls and ceiling, crouches down to touch the floor, confirming that all parts are there. He can feel all parts are there. But he cannot see them. In the undefined darkness, the passage could be a dancehall or funeral chamber. A columbarium or an abyss. Yet he has to trust what his hands blindly tell him. He cannot see to know.

I could light a match, he thinks. He does not light a match.

For a moment he considers turning back, going out the way he came in. For a moment, he wonders why he's even here. In this gap. In this state. The uncertainty threatens to overwhelm. But eventually that stops mattering to him. If what he seeks has never revealed itself to him in the light, he reasons, why wouldn't it then be revealed in the darkness?

He remembers his flight's arrival in the desert, the night's death-grip on this midnight country. He remembers the strip-mall ghost town outside the airport highway. Ben closes his eyes to what little light there is and calmly steps into the darkness.

"Ben?"

A hand on his shoulder. The rough kiss of stone on his cheek. Ben opens his eyes and finds El with him in the shade of a pointing finger of stone jutting from the canyon face. A cool breeze like a blue lost ribbon unspools through the ghost town while above, slipping like a yawn, the sun is easing into the west. He blinks and works his tongue to remove the taste of sleep from his mouth. Finally, he smiles at his cousin and pats the hand on his shoulder.

"G'morning."

"I thought I'd lost you out here." She leans as if to drop from her crouch to sit beside him, decides against it. "I found the cemetery, though. It's pretty nice."

He smiles at her, says nothing. He hasn't anything yet to say. In the brush below, a quail sees them and runs away spooked, then is simply running, aimless and zigging back and forth, already having forgotten what spooked it or that it was ever spooked.

"It's getting late," she says finally. "Did you want to see the graveyard?"

"No." He drawls the word while watching the bird as it finally disappears. "I think I found what I was looking for." Standing, leaning against the jutting stone, Ben fishes something from his pocket.

"What is it?"

In his hand, Ben holds a rusty chunk of broken shovel, like some strange jewel corroded and crumbling—"It's nothing"—and throws it down the rock face.

But this does not set well with El. She squints and looks down the slope to where the rusty bit tumbled and disappeared. She looks around at the shambled canyon and the tumbledown walls of the abandoned settlement, looks around where Ben imagines the cemetery might be. In the set of her mouth and the set of her shoulders, Ben can clearly read the question that's filling her, can cleary see how incapable he is of answering her with any amount of satisfaction, and tells her as much:

"I don't know, El. I just had to see for myself."

"See what, Ben?"

"What these people built." He covers his face with one hand when he speaks. "What they labored so hard for just so they could leave it behind. I guess maybe see if they fought to keep it or just walked away." Embarrassed, he picks a stone from the talus and tosses it down the slope. He bites his lip, almost hard enough to bleed. "I guess that's not something you can really see though, huh?"

Because the sun is behind him now, El's face is a peering squint. Less like she's trying to see through the light. More like she's trying to see into the dark. But she doesn't say anything and he hasn't anything else to say, so together they walk down the sloping scree.

Heading back through the canyon to the Jeep, El points to the twin narrow slots—the gaping blind eyes—cutting through the rock face. "What are those, do you think?"

"There's nothing in there." Ben doesn't look up to where she points. "Just a loop full of shadows."

"You went inside there?"

And like a poet or priest reciting, arms gesticulating in the air, "I walked straight into the mystery of its heart, to where no light has ever shone." He drops his arms limply to his sides. "I didn't see a thing."

THE SUN IS JUST setting when Ben drops off El at her house. Everything is a black shape against the red and purple sky, each tree and roofline melting into everything else. Somewhere between Fernley and Sparks, El decided that she would cook dinner for him—"In celebration of your arrival and acceptance," she said, "into America's foremost bastion for pointless endeavors"—so Ben rushes back to the 777 and showers, shaves off the patchy black scruff cropping up along his cheeks and under his chin.

He tries calling his friend in Boca. His friend in Boca never picks up the phone.

Wrapped in a towel and sitting on the corner of his bed, Ben writes for a while in his two notebooks—clinical details of the trip in his orange journal, more personal responses in the black—then tears open the envelope he'd found earlier waiting for him at the motel's front desk. Syracuse postmark concealing the stamp of a raven before a paling yellow hillscape. The slight weight of it in his hands makes him feel a little sick. The letter from his employers is brief. Just a quote from the *Agamemnon—the Helmsman lays it down as law...*—followed by a question about mercury in the water. Reading the letter over again, Ben feels certain: their query isn't seeking a response. They want his focus elsewhere.

To Sleep as Animals

In the letter's lower right-hand corner, he draws a rough sketch of the twin gaps in the rock face. The dead eyes of a cartoon skull. The open mouths of any gambling machine. Ben shakes the dust from his jacket and dresses, heads back to his Jeep.

On his way back to El's house, he stops at a Turkish café for an espresso and then a cognac, watches the men in their open-necked shirts, the women in their strappy dresses, everyone's expectant white teeth and eyes. All the world can be observed, he thinks, in how two people are drawn together then fall apart. Each example is the same as every other. Two bodies collide in a close orbit and feel good, only later to draw away and feel bad. While they're together, each gazes at the other and smiles. But really, they're only seeing the mirror of the other's face. At a pharmacy next door, Ben buys two bottles of wine even though El told him to bring nothing but himself and his innate childlike sense of play. Ben doubts he has such a thing—hence the cognac, hence the wine—in many ways is terrified by this fact, that he lacks something crucial that everyone else does not. Yet he knows better than to challenge El on this account.

"You need to stop thinking so seriously," she told him on the drive back from Ophir. "Because this version of adulthood you've adopted? It does *not* seem like much fun. I can tell by the way you walk. I've been studying you. You walk like a bull using its mind for horns. You need to stop leading with your head all the time, Ben, analyzing every step you take. Lead with your heart once in a while. Lead with your belly."

He lets himself inside El's house without knocking. Stringing through the rooms from unseen speakers, soft strange music quietly plays as if through a laudanum fog. A low voice made raw with whiskey and cigarettes. The smell of roast meat and dark fruit. The warmth of golden light. Ben finds El in the kitchen.

"Hey, you're here!" She's working at something at the kitchen's island counter, beaming warmly in a black dress that shows off her freckled shoulders. She sets down the bowl and spoon she's been working in her hands and comes around the corner to greet him, to hug him and touch his hair and take the bottles from him. "You shouldn't have."

"It's the least I could do." But he's trying to put something together. Between when she saw him and when she took the bottles from his hands, something happened—a flash, a feeling—something happened and he cannot say what it was.

"No, I mean it." She's standing with her back to him, a bottle in each hand, between the counter and fridge. "I told you not to." She glowers at him, one-eyed, over her shoulder. But her scolding is a joke, a form of play. Everything about her, Ben thinks, eventually becomes a form of play.

"One is a carménère," he says, "from up on the south face of one of these mountains." He almost has it figured out, this flashing mystery. "The other's an almond wine from Modesto." But it's gone.

She puts one bottle in the refrigerator and the other on the counter. From an already-open bottle, she pours him a glass and refills her own.

"To the great black hole of the past," she says, raising her glass—which seems to Ben like an odd thing to drink to—"where all our failures disappear."

Meeting her eyes, Ben touches his glass to hers. "Amen." And without looking away, they drink.

El decides he needs another tour of the house. It's been too long since his last visit to Nevada, she calims, and when here the other day, all he did was sleep. So while dinner takes care of itself in the oven, she leads him through her home. The living room with its umber couch and chair, its oak coffee table and few pictures on the walls, mostly small paintings and framed photographs but on one wall a large photograph of a silhouette figure framed by a brightly lit door as if walking from a dark room into a bright one. The tiled bathroom like a clean, efficient Roman space. The bedroom with its black-spread bed and moss-green walls. The office choked with papers and open files all pouring off of and hiding what might have once been a desk and computer.

"This was the room you stayed in last time," she says. "I traded your bed for a mess."

"Makes sense." On one wall is a poster of a bisected cow. "I often think I've done the same thing." But before he's expected to explain: "What is this music, anyway?"

"It's a record I found recently. About how Lewis Carroll fell in love with a young girl. It's like Wonderland is where his heart went to die."

"It sounds like it's made," he says, "by someone who has only heard descriptions of music but hasn't ever heard songs before."

"I think it's beautiful." But by her posture and by her tone, she seems to be agreeing with him. "I think it's a heartbreaking scenario."

And Ben nods. "Me too." But he doesn't know what he's agreeing to.

THEY DRINK BEN'S carménère with dinner. Wild rice and roasted asparagus and spiced pork wrapped in lime leaves, which Ben at first mistakes as edible but quickly learns are not. "They're for flavor," El explains, laughing as he spits a torn leaf back onto his plate. "They infuse the meat without coarsening it." It had never occurred to Ben to cook with leaves.

After dinner, they open the almond wine, which is thick and sweet but ferocious in its intensity. Ben imagines a green dragon coiled at the bottom of the bottle and says so, feeling embarrassed at the stupidity of the words as he says them, but El nods, examining the bottle and its label, not so much reading as simply seeing as she turns it in her hands.

"Yes, something with six legs and two tendrils like a mustache at the end of its snout." And now it seems like she's staring through the glass. "A thing that swims through the sky instead of flying. Like a demon and angel all at once." Ben watches the slim green thing slither from the bottle's mouth and into the kitchen's gold air, and after a dreamy silence, El laughs. "Oh lord, I'm drunk."

And Ben laughs too. "You are."

"I am. Oh no!"

"It's okay," he assures her, grinning. "We're in this together."

Covering her mouth with one hand like that might contain her laugher, El excuses herself to use the bathroom. While she's gone, Ben carries the dishes to the sink, takes his wine glass into the living room in a secret attempt to find where the music is coming from, but forgets his mission almost immediately and instead inspects the tiny pictures on the walls. The paintings are all details of small objects—the cracked grain of a walnut shell, the worm-eaten veins of a leaf, drops of oil like swimming eyes floating on a surface of water—rendered only in two or three colors and fixed to blocks of wood. The photographs are mostly old and faded yellow. Black-and-whites and sepia-tones. Long dead people and places that no longer exist.

When El returns, Ben is standing before the picture of the silhouette man in the door. "I hadn't noticed this before," Ben says when she comes to stand beside him, "but this guy in the picture, he's looking out from the frame, straight ahead into this room. Before, I thought he was looking the other way, walking away from us, but no. You can tell by the thin bit of light shining on his shoulder and his hair and cheek. He's looking out of the picture at us." He pauses to sip his wine and think this over. El watches him, saying nothing. "But he's also looking into a dark room. To us it looks like a dark figure standing before a door full of light, but he's looking into a dark room where something—us, a camera, everything outside the picture—is looking back at him. We can see him, but he can't see us. We're the darkness in the room." And he gestures in a way that takes in everything outside the picture frame. "Everything is the darkness of that room."

In the following silence, he realizes that at some point when he wasn't paying attention, the music around them has changed, has become something sparser but more dynamic, each instrument taking its turn to play just one note in the overall sequence, then waiting for its turn to come again. Yet above the sprawling jerkiness, the same ragged voice rises like a wave.

"It's a picture of you," she finally says. "I took it one time when Mum and I flew east to visit. This was the night you graduated from college."

For a while more, they stand before the picture, stand while Ben stares at himself, sees himself as El once saw him. Then El has his arm in hers, and at first he thinks she's being sentimental but no, she's twisting it, is laughing and trying to pin his arm behind his back. They grapple for a moment in the living room, laughing and pushing and nearly tripping over the coffee table before El challenges him to an arm-wrestling match.

"What?"

"What's the matter? Scared you'll be beat by a girl?" She's bouncing on the balls of her bare feet, fists up like she's ready to box.

"How old are you, like twelve?"

"C'mon, tough guy."

They arm wrestle at the kitchen table. Ben's surprised how strong she is. She almost beats him with her right arm and absolutely pins him with her left.

"It's like we're equal." He drinks the last of the almond wine from his glass. "We balance each other."

"Yeah, equal." She's red-faced and panting with laughter. "Except that I'm always going to be taller." And she wags a finger at him. "Nothing you can do about that."

"Don't be stupid. Height has no advantage in arm wrestling."

So they Indian leg wrestle, in which height has a definite advantage: push aside the coffee table and leg wrestle on the living room floor, lying hip-to-hip and toe-to-head. Ben wins the first match, forces her leg down to her chest and rolls her over onto her shoulders, so her dress comes up and he looks away. But in the rematch she clobbers him and in the next two bouts it becomes clear to Ben that she let him win the first time. They're laughing and gasping on the floor and somehow now much drunker than before and when Ben suddenly finds El on top of him, giggling with her mouth close to his, it's not all that much of a surprise.

Her mouth tastes like almonds. Her mouth tastes like limes.

The music turns and lilts and fills with horns and a wine-cracked falsetto. Ben has no idea how much time passes. Eventually they're wrestling again, pushing and twisting, each trying to achieve a victory both indistinct and fleeting. For a moment Ben thinks her mouth was something accidental and now forgotten—a thought that he finds somehow both an ache and a relief—but then things blur and when they again coalesce they are in El's bed and they're naked, and though there's still an element of play and of wrestling, the stakes feel raised. As if something more serious is tying their hands to one another, their mouths, their legs.

El's eyes meet Ben's eyes and for a moment things clarify and he sees exactly what they're doing, yet when he opens his mouth he hears himself asking where the music is coming from, and just as she tells him that there is no music, he's inside her, she gasps and just barely smiles but her eyes do not move away from his and he cannot take his eyes off hers, as he moves within her and her hands and legs move over him, drawing him in, he cannot take his eyes off hers until finally her eyes close and her limbs tighten in a knot around him and he empties himself inside her, and like a spring thunderstorm rending the air, the darkness is on him and he sleeps. Deep and instant sleep, drunk and coital. But in a moment he's awake again, is on his side and she's on her side with one leg thrown over his hips and he is still inside her. Beneath the blanket, she's petting his neck and petting his hair, the sweat cooling on his skin, and with calm eyes and a calm child's mouth she says over and over again, "Cousin…cousin…cousin…."

LATE IN THE NIGHT, in the darkness before dawn and the darkness of her room, he figures it out. "You kissed my mouth," he whispers. But she doesn't wake to hear. "When I came in. You said my name and kissed my mouth, then took the bottles from my hands." It's the last thing he remembers before he shudders into sleep. The repetition of her mouth. The repetition of her breath. Then even this is gone.

Chapter 4

ONCE WHEN BEN WAS very young, he dreamed he lived in a tumbledown mansion like a rickety maze fallen to degradation. Every floorboard wailed like a wounded animal, each step a rabbit with its paw caught in a trap. All the windows rattled in the wind. When they worked at all, the light bulbs flickered in the dark.

Ben lived in this house with his parents. His father a burly, dull-eyed thing like a sweaty shaved bear, yellow teeth and dirty jeans that sagged horribly from his hips. A glowering, surly thing. His mother a skeleton in a housedress. A ghost haunting itself, tearful smile and eyes lost in painted-on shadows. Though the distinction would not occur to Ben until much later, these people bore nearly no resemblance to the mom and dad he knew outside of dreams. He did his best to love these broken people, to accept how their minds had been crippled by obscure tragedies. He tried his best to love them. But he had good cause to not like them much at all.

Days came and went and the snow piled up higher against the peeling rotted siding of the house. An ever-expanding plain of blinding white, though the sky above was always impenetrable with night. As if the sun never rose, or something blotted the sky.

The snow buried all the first story windows. The snow crept up the second floor glass.

In the kitchen, his mother leaned against the table, staring intently at something Ben could never see. Reflected in the dull tabletop sheen. Hanging in the cool dead air. Beyond or through any wall or child.

In the cellar, his father furiously labored. A naked light swinging by a wire from the ceiling. A workbench made of a broken door laid between two creaking sawhorses. Torches and wrenches. The constant low murmur of curses and snarls.

Ben stayed away from the kitchen. Ben stayed out of the cellar.

In a vague hour of morning identical to any hour of night within the shudder and moan of this snowbound house, Ben woke and found his sheet wet and sticky, gluing itself to his pajamas and his pajamas to his legs. The stain was warm as a fever dream. His bed smelled like meat and honey.

Not knowing what had happened or what he'd done, Ben hid his soiled pajamas in shame, stuffed them in a ball under his mattress and made his bed as if nothing had happened. He took a bath before joining his parents for breakfast. He tried to forget the wet scent and heat in his bed.

But if his father's lumbering body was a bear's, his nose was of a fox. His father sniffed out what he'd done. Teeth bared and spitting, his father dragged Ben into his room by the collar of his shirt. Peeled back the blankets and pointed at the stain. Grey like mucus and marbled with veins. He lifted Ben like a hammer and pounded Ben's face into what he'd done.

And as he ground Ben's nose and mouth into the mattress, his father roared, "Never never never never…."

Ben lost a tooth to the stain. His nose sprayed blood like a fountain.

All the while, through the creak and groan of their trapped-animal home, Ben could hear his mother's wail. Her sorrow like a ripped-apart sheet. Her sorrow a voice lost in a well.

As a perfect compliment to the bear-in-father's-clothes, his mother's love was an act of violence, too. When Ben later wandered downstairs to the kitchen, dirtied and bleeding and dazed to the glassy blacks of his eyes, his mother pulled him to her where she sat at the kitchen table, pressed his face into her shoulders and breasts and neck, cried into his hair and into his ears until they rang, squeezing him until his body bent and his bones seemed ready to pop or crack free. When he fought against her, her hands became claws. She screamed. Pinned in place with his hips between her knees—his mother's hooking hands patting his head in long, hard strokes—Ben gave himself up to her needy affection until she tired and set him free.

His mother's skin smelled like cigarettes and coffee, stale and acrid and biting. His father smelled of onions and old meat.

Most of his time Ben spent wandering among the house's many rooms. While his parents argued in the kitchen, while his father fought his imagination with torch and tool in the basement and his mother sought out some recognizable shape among the dead spaces in the air, Ben patiently explored their home. It did not occur to him that he was seeking a way out. He thought he was seeking only something new. But none of the lights in any room ever worked, would ever turn on. He was always left to wonder what was going on in the darkness, in the shadows beyond his sight.

Outside, the blinding white reached toward the roof, toward the horizon, toward the sky.

Ben stopped sleeping under the covers, slept fully dressed on top of his bed. His father had told him to clean up his mess, but he had not obeyed. The stain had begun to grow and move, and it pulsed as if it were breathing or had a beating heart. Sometimes it made gurgling or cooing sounds. Ben didn't want to clean up what he had made.

Once while wandering among the rooms and groaning halls, Ben found a window open. Its faded curtains flapping gossamer in a cold wind. The snow sifting in like morning noises in a dream. He stood before the window and wondered why it was open, whose hands had raised the glass. Outside, everything was seamless beneath the sky's opaque black. No tracks in the snow. No distant lights or distant trees. As if beyond the wind-rocked walls of this house, all the rest of the world was gone. As if this were the entirety of the earth. Everything ended beyond this glass. Shivering, Ben slammed the window shut.

Eventually the stain broke free of the sheet and became its own creature, small and rubbery with six legs like a mantis and a body shaped like a compound tadpole, a patchwork of soft lumps and tails and razor-stiff limbs, its eyes like oil-drops on dirty dishwater, its mouth an oval grin.

Ben didn't tell his parents about the creature. He did his best to stay out of their way. He avoided their hands and eyes.

The creature grew quickly and learned to walk and run. Ben fed it gel-covered processed meat hunks from unlabeled cans in the pantry. Sometimes the way the creature ate its food—its oval grin working in a measured rhythm, oil-drop eyes fixed firmly on Ben's—or how it glistened in the light repulsed Ben. But watching it learning to solve puzzles, learning to perform graceful yet useless motions with its six limbs like butterfly knives, Ben also felt a growing affection for the thing.

Ben thought of his father bashing his face bloody into the stain, his commands of never, his entire being—his voice, his posture—a punishment for the boy. He thought of his father's rotten breath and yellow, sneering teeth. Ben decided he would keep the creature.

The snow swallowed the second story windows. The snow crept toward the attic.

The creature grew and learned and developed a language of its own, one Ben could not understand. Just coos and purrs. The creature got frustrated with Ben's blatant lack of comprehension and stopped talking to him. For days, the room became an uncomfortable, silent cell. Like any other wing of the house.

Then the creature laid an egg.

At this point, the creature was hardly bigger than a cat. Its egg was the size of Ben's fist. The creature laid the egg in a mucousy mess on top of Ben's pillow, sniffed at it once, then turned away.

Ben tried to coax it into caring for the egg, but the creature ignored his pleading shouts and flapping hands. When Ben tried to pick up the creature and set it on the egg, it bit his hand hard enough to draw blood.

Ben dropped the creature and sucked his wounded hand. The creature stared with its oval grin open. In its impassive black eyes, Ben could not tell if it loved him or hated him. And maybe it didn't matter. Love or hate, it didn't care if it hurt him. He knew: it would do it again. Ben gathered the egg and took his lamp from the nightstand and moved to another room. He locked the door from the outside when he left.

On an earlier excursion into the house's many rooms, Ben found one—using his hands, using his fingers—that had once been a bedroom. A night table and a desk and a mattress made up on a metal frame. Ben set his lamp on the night table, plugged it in and turned it on, set the egg softly on the bed.

Ben understood how this worked. The heat of the greater warms through the nutshell of the lesser. Crawling under the covers, Ben wrapped himself around the egg, and though he felt himself warming within his clothes beneath the blankets, the egg seemed to be cooling beside him. So he got out of bed and took off his clothes and got back in, wrapping himself around the egg like an oyster to a pearl, passing his heat from skin to shell, and after dozing for a while he woke to find the egg hatched open and his naked oyster limbs wrapped around the pearl of an old woman.

Her skin was soft and loose and warm. Her hand was tender on his cheek.

Ben told the woman his name and explained to her about the creature and about the egg. She in turn explained to him that she was his grandmother. But she didn't use words he knew. She spoke in hums and spoke in whirs. But still, he knew who she was and what she meant. He'd have recognized his grandmother anywhere.

The noise in the cellar was growing louder, more fierce, the snarl of tools and the snarl of his father. The creature clattered around in its room, the sounds of its flailing growing in step with the growth of its body behind the locked-shut door. Ben found clothes for his grandmother and found things for her to eat. Mostly pages from waterlogged books and dried rose hips from a canning jar he found on a shelf.

She taught Ben to hum and taught him to whir. She taught him games using bits of finger-smoothed bone, or using logic, or using his body. Sometimes they'd sit on the bed and just stare at one another, memorizing the details of the other. Sometimes they slept tied like wind-knotted clothes on a line. And on the night the creature broke down its door and his father emerged from the cellar, horrible and victorious with his invention, he did not fear the wrath either carried, stalking for him through unlit stairs. In the warm welcome of his grandmother's love, he was pacified by the knowledge that he was his grandmother's grandfather. What he made and what had made him could not hurt him. In this cycle, they were all the same thing. An axis of light and an axis of darkness, each working a balanced design. The howl of beasts thrashing in the dark. His grandmother's skin on his skin. He was saved.

IN THE CLEAN WHITE world of daylight, Ben's parents did not want to hear about this dream. The first time he told them—that next morning over cereal and milk and tall glasses of orange juice—

his mom and dad listened in a shocked sort of silence. But later, they would not listen. They'd cut off his retelling. They'd ask he not retell it again.

But Ben was hard pressed to do as his parents asked. He could not stop thinking of the dream. Of the grandmother hatched from an egg. Of his accidental creature. He spent silent hours sprawled on the living room floor, construction paper and crayons cast around him in a fan. He memorialized each detail of the dream in picture. He created his memory's photographs.

When he talked of his dream now, he no longer spoke of it as a dream.

This is when his dad took Ben aside and gave him the rules for proper conduct. "I don't want you to be the weird kid at school," his dad said, smiling despite the obvious sorrow in his eyes. "That kid that no one likes. I want you to succeed at being a kid."

So Ben put on the mask of his parents' expectations and pretended it was his true skin, did the best he could to be the way they wanted him to be. Even when he saw he was failing. Even when he knew he would never succeed.

Chapter 5

THE CALLS FINALLY return. Ben drives up to Boca—through the thinned-out desert waste and into California, into the giant shaggy pines of the upward mountain slope—to visit his glass-artist friend.

It turns out the number he'd been calling was essentially wrong, rang to the office at Alex's studio, not to his home. While bulldozing through the weekly paperwork that morning, Alex saw the flashing red eye of the answering machine winking at him, and within a few hours, Ben was on his way.

He had gotten the call while in the Peppermill's dim casino lounge, enjoying an eye-opener and interviewing an old woman named Ethyl who had once been a dancer at any number of clubs around the city but who now was retired on the money she'd saved and the money she earned playing blackjack and keno and the occasional slot machine. "A lot of girls get sucked up into a particular lifestyle when they're dancing," she told him, smoking a long flavored cigarette and rattling the ice in an oily-looking vodka drink in the moody twilight of the casino lounge. "I knew better. From the start, I knew better. Seems to me sometimes like I'm the only one who ever did know better, too. All the girls I knew then and all the girls I know now, they all blow their money on waxing their crotches and augmenting their tits or asses. I knew one girl who had the muscle in her forehead snipped so she wouldn't get wrinkles there. Knew more than one who did that. Now they all always look surprised. I always exercised and ate right and shaved my own crotch the old-fashioned way. I never got involved with a client unless I knew he was safe. Harmless but lonely men willing to pay to not feel so alone." Ethyl's voice was the wet rip of old jeans tearing in two. Between the few lines on her face and the lounge's black-lit gloom, Ben had no idea how old she might be. "A few decent men took care of me for a while, but to no greater degree than I wanted them to. It began and ended when I said so. No man ever lorded over me or dragged me from the stage or got me pregnant or in any way turned me into anything I didn't want to be. I was the one in control." She blew out smoke like it were some sort of curse and stabbed out her cigarette in the ashtray. "Which is more than I can say about most of the dancers I've known. Most girls give it away to anyone. It's like they want their lives destroyed. Like it's all they deserve."

This was when Alex called. Finishing his drink and paying for Ethyl's, Ben thanked her for her time and her story, then asked if he could take her picture. Which seemed to surprise her. Yet she agreed. Ben did not use the word *evidence* in his question. She smiled and tossed her hair, posed with one elbow propped on the bar, one hand on her still-round hip. But in the black lights gleam—from among the bottles, off the mirror and polished bar—the viewfinder revealed only a dark human shape impressed against the iridescent backdrop, a violet reptile sheen where her eyes were supposed to be. Which was fine by Ben. Perfect. He finished taking his notes on Ethyl behind the wheel of his parked Wagoneer, then headed up the mountainside highway to Boca.

ALEX IS TALL AND muscled as a sailor with a crooked mess of teeth. Just as Ben remembers him. He greets Ben at the studio door with a painful embrace and a bottle of cheap bourbon. They hug and grin in each other's faces and slap one another on the head, pull a long drink from the bottle, head inside through the studio door.

"I have a little bit of work left to do today," Alex says, "before I can send my boys home and enjoy myself in my own right. I'm sure you don't mind sticking around for a spell?"

"It'd be my pleasure. It's been too long since I last saw you work."

Leading him through the gallery toward the hot shop, Alex smiles his junkyard grin over his shoulder at Ben. On either side of them as they pass through, life-size glass women, voluptuous and variously posed, cloister in the gallery space. The swell of hips and cleft of sex. Ben stops and stares, lays his hand over his face—

"I think you'll enjoy watching this new piece come around."

—then follows his friend into the hot shop.

Two other men are waiting by the shop's gigantic blast furnaces when Ben and Alex come in, standing like guardians or soldiers with their goggles and gloves and punty rods raised like javelins at the ready. As Alex joins his team, Ben finds a safe corner from which to watch.

This was how Ben and Alex met, in a glass shop much like this at their college in New York State. Ben stood stupefied in the middle of the glass studio floor, agog and staring at the unwinking white eye of the glory hole, the glowing-orange gathers of glass the other students spun and shaped at the end of their punties, the mastodon furnaces roaring throughout the vast hall. It was while Ben was standing stupefied that Alex came up behind him, picked him up, gently set him out of the way as a graduate student came through with a massive glass oyster upraised on a punty and aimed for the glory hole. Ben watched while the team finished the sculpture, then stepped forward to apologize for being in the way, offering to buy them all a drink. Only Alex took him up on the offer.

While Alex dons a pair of heavy gloves and deeply-tinted goggles, one of his assistants gathers a large blob of glass from a crucible and brings the punty to Alex, who takes it to what looks like a modified weight bench and sets it across the flat horizontal arms, keeping the rod spinning so the molten-orange glass doesn't drip. With steel tweezers and a wide rectangular knife, Alex shapes the glass until from the hunk emerges a soft contour of belly, a double up-swell of breasts, ridges of collarbone and shoulder blade. Periodically, he brings the form back to the superheated mouth of the glory hole, keeping the glass hot and malleable. His voice an occasional low grunt of command. Sweat dripping from his forehead and nose.

And as the hot glass spins—its navel transfixed on the punty's tip—gravity's constant hand bends and shifts the body, making it move as if it were alive and writhing. Eventually, Alex's assistants bring more molten glass from the crucible and together the three men form arms and legs. As the overall form coalesces into something recognizable and feminine, Alex carves in muscle-tone and definition with small knives and steel tongs, sometimes attaching pellets of cold glass that his assistants blast with a gigantic torch—its magnesium white flame as long as Ben's arm—until soft and glowing.

When the body's done, the assistants take it to a heat garage to keep it from cooling too quickly while Alex takes another gather of glass with his punty rod and with knife strokes too quick for Ben to fully register, carves from the glass a woman's face. Beautiful and sad and somehow familiar. Alex adds a little more glass for the hair and cheekbones, but in just a few deft movements, he's made the face he wanted.

The assistants bring back the body and, just a few minutes later, the head and body are fused together and the punties are broken free with water and methodical taps of a butcher's knife. The two assistants hold the detached body like it's the most dangerous infant in the world. The finished woman looks beautiful and terrified. All grace and defense. As if uncertain as to whether she's enjoying this game or not.

Taking off his gloves and clapping them together like a flat, cracking bell, Alex directs his assistants as to what to do with this new finished woman before they cut out early for the day. Then he reconvenes with Ben and the bottle and they each have another drink.

"That was amazing." Ben can smell the sweat and hot furnace sulfur pouring off Alex in a choking cloud. "That didn't take you any time at all."

"I might have done this once or twice." Alex takes another pull from the bottle, then smells himself under the arm and winces. "Jesus. Let's go for a swim."

THEY LEAVE BEN'S Wagoneer at the studio and drive up to the Boca Reservoir in Alex's rattling rust-heap of a pickup. As they pull away from the studio, Ben notices a stack of pipes and hoses and what looks like rocket engines tucked around the corner of the shop.

"What's that there?"

"Used to be a kiln." Alex doesn't look up as he swings the truck onto the road and down the hill.

"Natural gas." The engine trembles and dies. Unflinching, Alex throws it in neutral, turns the ignition and pumps the gas until the engine roars back to life. "For firing ceramics. Used to, anyway." And he grins cryptically. "Now it fires nuclear bombs."

Along the way, they stop at a log-hewn mercantile and each grab a couple deuces of some local microbrew. Throughout the rest of the ride to the reservoir—with his giant bottle of brown ale open and the truck shivering like a dying mule over every pothole and rut as Alex, sweaty and dirty, glowers pirate-eyed through the dusty windshield grime—Ben keeps trying to wake himself, keeps falling into the pattern of drifting off while in transit. Even though he's enjoying himself. Even though he wants to be awake. He has to keep wresting himself from some vague animal dream.

"What the hell are you doing over there?"

"Huh? Nothing. Just a little jittery."

"You look like you're killing black flies." Alex pulls long from his beer. "Lots of 'em. Fucking quit it."

Ben rolls down his window and lets the wind blow his eyes awake.

FROM WHERE THE ROAD deposits them, the reservoir looks like a gigantic crater half-filled with water, a long, high ridge dividing the beach from the rest of the world. They ride along the crater's rim where a scattering of other cars are parked. As if oblivious to this detail, Alex plows his truck off the edge, down the slope and slamming to the gravel below.

"Jesus Christ, man!"

The suspension crunches sickeningly like a dozen empty paint cans tumbling down a fire escape.

"What? What happened?" But Alex is already out the door and heading for the water, stripping to his shorts and diving in.

Flying kites or tending small fires: a few people broadcast along the water's edge. All of them stopped and staring. Unilateral disapproval. Finishing his beer, Ben strips out of his clothes and he joins his friend in the water.

"I THINK IT'S PRETTY obvious that we're not supposed to swim here."

Alex handstands under water, then comes up snorting like a bear.

"That's what's great about California. Plenty of laws, but no enforcement. Lets us look civilized without actually having to act that way."

But Ben's wondering what would happen if he or Alex began to drown out here. If either would help the other or simply stand back and watch, more curious than concerned. Wonders if anyone on shore would notice or care. This dark edge has always run through their friendship: Ben felt its return as soon as he walked into Alex's studio, as soon as he heard his voice over the phone. A barely contained storm of nihilism rages beneath Alex's skin—Ben's always believed that—and that storm is contagious. Even his acts of creation—all fire and melting—feel like acts of destruction. As Alex dives again, Ben wonders if he should hold him under, push against him until there's nothing left to push against.

When Alex rises to the surface, leaping from the water, he's a shark with ruined teeth.

To Sleep as Animals

THEY CLIMB FROM THE water and sip their beers while lying in the gravel, drying in the sun. Then they play frisbee for a while, whipping the disc for what seems to Ben to be unfathomable distances up and down the beach until someone's yellow lab charges through and snatches the frisbee out of the air and runs, hard and fast and proud with its prize as it disappears over the reservoir rim. "If that ain't a sign," Alex intones, shielding his eyes against the sun to see where the dog has gone, "I don't know what is." They pack into the truck, roar over a low spot in the crater's lip, finish their beers on the road to Alex's house.

AT THE END OF A TWISTED scratch of dirt road, Alex's house is a timber-frame tower surrounded by stands of mammoth Ponderosa pine and Douglas fir. Dead red needles like porcupine quills litter the ground underfoot. Birds twitter and scuffle between trees. As far as Ben can tell, almost no one else lives out this way.

Alex fills two tall glasses with crushed ice and bourbon and they settle around a table parked on the back deck, playing cards in the pine-dappled afternoon light, obscure games from Eastern Europe or the Middle East, games only Alex knows the rules for and very well might be making up as he goes along. While they play, amid half-jokes and one-liners, Ben briefly recaps his stay in the desert so far.

"You're researching ghost towns and hanging out with homeless dudes?"

"I don't think I see it really as two distinct things."

"Are you familiar," he asks, "with the term *pendejo*?"

But before Ben can answer, Alex finishes his drink and stands from the table, card game clearly over, and goes to start a too-large fire in his barbecue pit. Drowns some hunks of meat in sauce. Tosses them hissing onto the grill.

They drink beers and watch the smoke curl and eddy from their dinner. They eat with their hands while kicking a soccer ball around the yard.

It's a strange and secret process that turns the day into night, one where neither Ben nor Alex notices the fleeting light until it's gone and night's upon them with its silver disc of moon and marauding hoards of mosquitoes. They savor the coolness of night as long as the parasites will allow.

Once inside, something suggests to Alex that it's a party now, so he puts some sort of industrial pop music on the stereo and plays it loud, begins dancing around the house with his hands in the air and bare feet sliding across the hardwood floor. And watching, foolish grinning, from the corner of the room, Ben realizes that this was what college was like—the booze and half-assed attempts at sports, the card games and instant dance parties—and that he's legitimately happy to be reliving it with Alex. He knows how he should feel and feels it. Even as Alex approaches with thrusting hips and an over-erotic "O" of mouth, gyrating in circles around Ben to this ridiculous music.

"Oh, oh. Ah yeah!"

He knows how he should feel and feels it.

Eventually Alex puts on something more listenable and crashes onto a couch. They finish the remaining beers while blathering at length about whatever, and Ben is still happy with this resubmergence into his past life, but when the beer runs out and they start in on a plastic bottle of cheap Scotch, something changes in Alex, and like the progression from day into night, Ben doesn't notice until it's too late.

"I don't know what to do, man," Alex sobs, and the sheer fact that this man is crying—this man who bends fire and glass to his will, who eats charred meat barehanded and decides what rules and laws do and do not apply to him—causes Ben to doubt the reality of this situation. He was waxing nostalgic via muscle memory with this friend, but this is something different. Someone changed the rules of the game, leaving even Alex in the lurch. Having no idea what's brought this on, Ben sits back and does his best to memorize the absurdity of this scenario, makes his brain into a map of a crying man.

Eventually, he realizes that this is about a woman.

"It just tears me up, the things she does to herself, you know, 'cause I love her, I still love her after all these years and all the shit she's pulled. It's like she's somehow tied this invisible fucking rope to me, so no matter how free I feel or how far away I run, whenever she wants, man, she can reel me back in. I'm just some goddamn puppy on a string."

There's a pause where some sort of commiseration seems appropriate. So Ben does his best to commiserate.

"Fuck it, man," and he passes the bottle to his friend, "no woman's worth that."

"But she is, man, she is." There's something in the way he looks at Ben, peering around the bottle as he drinks. Liquid descending as bubbles rise. Something almost evil. "She is."

And though there's no reason for these pieces to click together, all at once Ben realizes who Alex is talking about, has maybe always known but didn't want to admit it. Because the girl he is crying for is someone Alex dated in college—over ten years ago—is someone Ben had known too and had even had sex with. He'd hiked up her skirt as she pressed her cheek to the dirty brick wall in an alley behind a frat bar. It smelled like piss and vomit back there. He wonders if Alex's infatuation goes back that far. All those years and all those nights. A dark-eyed girl who didn't care who he was. Ben fucked his friend's star-crossed love in a dirty frat-bar alley.

"I sometimes have this dream," Alex says.

"I had a dream one time—"

"—this dream where she and I are together. And we live in a nice house. And we have a couple kids. Then I catch her with some other guy. Or with a bunch of guys all at once. And even though I want to kill the bastards for doing what they're doing to her, I don't. I don't do anything. I just watch."

The way Alex is staring through the dead air of the room—as if the walls and the light and the dark pines beyond, the mountains and deserts and pinprick lights high up in the sky, as if everything were invisible or simply not there—fills Ben with a mounting sense of dread.

"Sometimes I see them all melting."

The way anything in a nightmare is terrifying.

"Like an atom bomb is burning off their skin."

The slow climb of a spider up its silk. The inevitable blink of an eye.

"Sometimes I'm burning with them."

Ben would do anything to make this conversation end. So he knocks over the bottle of Scotch, off the coffee table and onto the floor where it rolls away, puking over dirty hardwood and for a few minutes, the two of them stumble stooped-over with towels and dishrags, sopping up the mess. And though afterward things return to a more jovial sense of normalcy, Ben cannot help now but see his friend as a stranger, some sort of nostalgia machine twisting the past into a sad parody of itself. No lingering trace of their earlier old-friend camaraderie. Just two strangers killing time with one another as the night hours slip oily by.

Yet earlier, while Alex wrestled with the preparation of the grill and as the beer and bourbon gathered in a fuzzy gauze in the forefront of his brain, Ben wandered through the house in search of a bathroom and instead found Alex's private archive. A small dark room near the end of the hallway, door swollen tight in its frame, a heavy-curtained window inside letting in next to no light.

For a moment Ben stood framed in the doorway, staring into the dark room and not knowing if he should enter or just close the door. Not knowing how much of an intrusion old friends are allowed to make on one another. Not knowing what constitutes an intrusion. Through the gloom, he could make out vague blocky shapes and sheets of paper hanging from the walls. Ben switched on the light, stepped into the cramped room.

Most of the space was dominated by a large metal desk pushed against one wall, the sort of desk Ben remembered certain teachers having in school. Cool to the touch and screeching at the drawers, a reverberant boom whenever accidentally knocked into. Beside the desk stood two matching filing cabinets. On one wall hung a poster of Brancusi's *Endless Column* vanishing to a pinprick into the sky. On the other, an oversized portrait of who might have been Norman Mailer. In between, a window's repressed light made the curtains glow.

This should have been enough to satisfy Ben's curiosity: the private office of a friend, probably dedicated to a collection of celebrity photographs or to writing poetry or maybe simply to paying bills. But the two most visible articles on the desk's face—a black and white photograph of some seaside town taken from above, another of a beautifully ornate theater brightly lit in the night, well-dressed Asian people milling before the façade—drew Ben in. What had he found so far? What had he left to find? Leaning over the desk, Ben examined the loose stack of pictures.

Many were shots of what Ben presumed to be the same city: busy foot-trafficked streets, a boat pulling into the harbor, a tall pre-modern building impressed upon a clear sky, children playing near a pond in a park. One—possibly taken at the same theater or opera house—showed a beautiful woman, teeth gleaming and almond eyes alight as her upturned face beamed toward the night sky. At her side, a well-dressed man leaned in to kiss her softly on the neck. Another showed three figures in lab coats standing formally on the steps of some academic building. Yet another showed little more than sky and the corner of one rooftop, a silhouette bird, a vaporous cloud.

The final image was nearly identical to the first. A view from above. The entire seaside city. The only difference was a dark cigar shape in the lower right-hand corner, superceding the rest of the image like a thumb creeping over the lens: a bomb falling toward the city below.

Inside the filing cabinet, Ben found more pictures of what might have been the city's aftermath, blasted windows and the burnt-out hulls of blackened buildings, scattered rubble, bodies ripped apart and fused together by impossible recombinant heat. But really, this could have been anywhere. The predicted outcome of any modern siege, all organized in a folder labeled PRIMARY EVIDENCE. As far as Ben could tell, no other folder was labeled.

Other files contained black and white pictures of European cities—in Germany, Britain, France— similarly ripped asunder. Some held color photos of Eastern Europe or Africa, homes on fire and blue-and-white helmets, bodies stacked like firewood or dumped into trenches, limbs mangled and dusted in lye. All of which reminded Ben of his short-lived childhood baseball card collection. The various poses, the portraits and action shots. All the statistics a quantitative analysis of the execution of feats he didn't really care much about. He'd had no interest in the game or the players. Simply in the totality of the collection. As if by owning every piece to the game's puzzle, he might understand what it means.

When Alex finally called to him from the yard—to come witness the size of the centipede he'd just caught inside his upturned whiskey glass—Ben was flipping through a trio of images: Hirohito, Idi Amin, Pinochet, all microphoned or megaphoned before screaming crowds. Slipping the pictures back into their folder and sliding closed the drawer, Ben shut the room and, unbothered, returned to the company of his friend.

THERE ARE THREE guestrooms with nicely made beds and unused furniture, bright still with the scent of hand-chiseled cedar. There's a mosquito-screen tent out behind the garage with an Army cot and the earthy scent of pine needles swishing through the air. Yet Ben curls like a wounded dog on a portion of the couch while Alex sprawls snoring on the floor as softly through the radio, something bad is happening at Amanda's Saloon where sometimes the mescal is free.

In the morning, Ben wakes up before Alex, wanders out among the tall Ponderosas in the sweet cool scent of dawn. He listens to the songs of birds he cannot see and watches the erratic motions of those he can. He follows a set of animal prints until they disappear in a drift of dead needles. He does his best to melt the ache in his head into the ache of the unconscious world and its laws of perpetual suffering and endurance, and when he walks back to Alex's, he sees that a bear got into the garbage sometime in the night. Shredded bags and food scraps everywhere. He takes a picture but back inside, he doesn't tell Alex about it.

BEN FORGETS THE contents of the pictures almost as soon as he sees them. Just shades of grey on glossy paper. But the image of Alex crying sticks with him like a worm in his belly.

Closing his eyes just sends the world spinning, but without a protective darkness or shade, the Monday morning light is a nightmare. They say nearly nothing on the drive out to the studio, their silence like a breach in an aircraft, sucking out the air, and unable to nod off while they ride, Ben is helpless but to witness. Something's changed between them in the hours since last night, something intangible but real. The sort of distance you're not likely to ever bridge again. Ben knows this feeling should be killing him, turning his stomach and heart. Ben knows exactly how he's supposed to feel.

In the gravel lot in front of the studio they mumble a sort of goodbye. Ben knows what Alex knows. With chances so great, how could they ever meet again?

Chapter 6

It doesn't take long for the grey men to find him. As if they'd waited days for his return. Pacing the parking lot. Squinting through the darkened windows of his room. They're waiting when he pulls in to the 777.

"Where've you been, Ben?" Earl asks him as he steps out of the Wagoneer, and as Ben turns to regard the half-eared man, he sees legitimate concern written in the bleary eyes. "We've been worried."

"Sorry, Earl." Ben locks the truck and grimaces in the sun. It was much cooler in the mountains. "I had work to do. Sometimes things get carried away."

"Well, we're just glad you're safe." In the mid-morning haze rolling off the parking lot pavement,

Earl steps forward to clap Ben on the back. "We're glad to have you home." And in a silent chorus, the grey men nod their accord.

FROM THE 777, THEY lead him down a side street and across the lawn of an abandoned house. Under a knifed-up tree and past a broken swing set. Into a garbage can alley that deposits them onto another sleepy street with plastic bags tangled around the feet of stop signs and little kids not so much playing as watching the day slowly bake away, their toys forgotten in the brown grass.

"By the way," Earl asks, "how's your cousin?"

Slowly, a beat up heap of a car drifts past, mariachi trumpet scales swaggering through the open windows. It feels like a tree bursting ridiculously into bloom. It feels like perfection.

"She's doing fine." And he smiles, squeezes his friend's shoulder. "Thank you for asking."

At the end of the block, they duck through a tear in a chain-link fence into a narrow gap between an apartment building and a bodega. Dusty bricks to one side, crackling stucco to the other. Halfway down, the grey men come to a halt and stand proudly around a garbage can.

"This is it?" Corrugated tin with a massive dent in the side. "This is what you wanted to show me?"

Grinning, Earl lifts the lid with a ridiculous flourish, revealing—under a scrap of newspaper, atop a squished bag of trash—a nest of nine bottles of vodka.

"There were more," Earl explains, "but we dipped into the stash."

Picking out a bottle, Ben reads the label. AUTHENTIC RUSSIAN VODKA. Distilled in Kenya. Bottled in plastic. Bearing a Scottish clan name. "Where'd you guys get this?"

"Zack did it." And they all point to the youngest of the group, not so much a grey man but a grey boy, a college kid who intended on hitchhiking across the United States on his summer off from school, but after crossing the Sierras and dropping down into the desert valley, decided he'd gone far enough.

"He was walking down the street Friday afternoon," Earl explains, "and he saw a box truck making a delivery in front of a liquor store. The big door in back of the truck was open, and since no one was around, he grabbed the first case he saw and ran. Didn't you, Zack?"

Beside him, Zack grins proudly at Ben. Scraggly beard and dirty spectacles. Crude faces tattooed on the tips of his fingers. Wooden earrings like boar tusks curling out of his lobes. Features so exaggerated as to make him almost beyond human, intensely human: flawed, dirty, reshaped by personal desire. Looking at this recovering academic, Ben can't help but feel proud, too.

"Nice job, boys." And they're all grinning now and proud. Broken teeth and ragged lips. "But we need a better hiding place than this."

"What, what's wrong with this?"

"Well, you might be good for a little while longer, but…. When does the trash go out on this street?"

And of course, no one answers. He should have known that no one would know.

"See, now this is the problem. You're forgetting your own rules. Your memory has to be a map." But he can tell they don't know what he's talking about. Whatever wisdom a night's bottle brings is immediately erased by another sleepless dawn, another quarter begged, another bullshit epiphany found swirling in another night's bottle. So obvious. But Ben fell for it. He'll be damned if he gives it up. "You'd all be pissed if this went out in the back of a garbage truck. This is your windfall. You can't lose it all at once. Help me get these out of here."

Bashful for their upbraiding, they each hide a bottle or two down a pant leg or in a jacket sleeve and follow Ben the half-dozen blocks to the popped-loose sewer grate he found on his second day in town. A mouth that can only leer out from the pavement. Like Alex's junkyard grin.

"Keep a look out, will you." Ben squints down the street. "I already have one cop looking out for me. The last thing I need is another friend."

Kneeling on the pavement, Ben carefully slips the bottles through the curb access and onto the concrete ledge within. Toy soldiers in formation in the under-street gloom.

"I don't imagine," he says, dusting off his knees as he stands, "we have to worry about a heavy rain washing these away. Now our stash is hidden, easily accessible, and in no danger of going out with the trash. And if one slips and rolls out of reach, a couple of you can muster together and lift open the grate."

The grey men huddle around him, humbled but proud. Only Zack seems fully pleased by these turning events, not knocked down at all, and for a moment Ben wonders about this kid's motivations for being tied up in this life, these men and these streets. A student who's given up on education, prideful when he's proven to have not learned. To have sought nothing and learned nothing in return. Ben considers his own participation with these men, on these streets, how potentially equal he might be to this grey boy with warthog tusks curving from his ears. He wonders at their shared agenda. Their shared goals. Zack just grins and grins.

A car goes by and then another. Two boys on one bicycle slowly roll past on the sidewalk. Earl asks Ben if he'd like to join them for a celebratory drink, and Ben would like to and nearly does, but it's then that the phone in his pocket begins its persistent buzz. Catherine. The post-grad botanist. Forager of the Tahoe snow plant.

"Sorry boys," and he holds up his vibrating phone. "Do people accept rain checks in the desert?"

"Cash only."

He leaves them kneeling in the gutter, someone's arm descending into the dark as he trots up the street, phone pressed to his ear.

CATHERINE IS ALREADY on her way to Tahoe when she calls, has to make a few stops in town before heading into the woods. "By the time you get here," she says, "I should be done with my errands and ready." She gives him directions to a trailhead just off of Route 50. She says she'll see him soon.

Back at the 777, Ben doesn't even bother with his room, just hops into his Jeep and leaves. He is beyond needing fresh clothes, he thinks. He's become something essential, pure and raw. Beyond any shower or shave. A dirty hungover man. He guides his Jeep south onto 395.

The day is revealing itself as a bright and searing new star, vaporizing and hot. Ben feels he's probably been warned about this. He peels off his jacket and rolls down the windows, drives to Tahoe in a deafening gospel of wind.

Though he can't see it, Ben knows when he's passed Hanover's Ophir Mill site. He can feel it sizzling behind him like fat on a griddle, dissolving into smoke. The whole desert rises up around him to dissolve into oily smoke.

Somewhere south of Carson City, Ben stops to pick up a hitchhiker, a weary-eyed middle-aged man who might be a vestigial hippie or maybe just another lost soul on a latter-day vision quest, a potential or recovering grey man. Tiny dreamcatcher pendant on a sweat-shined leather thong. A professional haircut gone to shag and a leather vest that was once a leather jacket. The faint scent of road dust and sun, the earthy scent of pot. They turn off 395 onto Route 50, head up into the mountains and listen to the wind's lupine hymn, and neither says a word.

Ben thinks of the people in the diner who say nothing over eggs and coffee. He thinks of his friends drinking whiskey to stave off Boston's cold. Remembers so deeply within the wind's howling psalm that it's like entering again the twin blind eyes in the canyon's face at Ophir Mill.

An amnesiac place with no light, no edges or plains to define. A blank spot in his memory unfurling like the petals of a massive black lily. No hitchhiker beside him. No miles filled with road. Nothing from the outside world reaching him inside this insular dark. Only this: an undefined absence of memory, a tenuous absence within himself. Then, just as suddenly—like flicking on a light, like the flash of police cruiser red and blues flagging him down in the night—he's back and the hitchhiker is asking to be let out. Already, they are halfway up the mountain. Ben has no idea how long he's been gone. In a moment, he forgets that he even was.

The man doesn't say anything when Ben draws to a stop along the highway shoulder, shakily gathering his bags and stepping out onto the road. Like something has just happened to him and he has to get away. Like something terrible is waiting up ahead. Ben wonders at his silently chosen path, where it leads to and from where it leads away. As the man drags himself up the road, Ben takes a picture of him through the dirty windshield glass.

To Sleep as Animals

OFF ROUTE 50 AND up a rough incline of cracked bedrock and moss-grown ruts—in the mountain cool of Ponderosa stands, calling birds and the soft burble of ditch water—Ben finds Catherine waiting under dense pine shade, arms folded over her chest and leaning against the hood of her old blue Ford. Surprised by her unwelcoming posture, Ben smiles warmly and shouts hello as he hops out of the Jeep.

"You're late," she replies. "By nearly two hours."

Which doesn't add up. Aside from picking up the hitchhiker, he drove straight here without a stop. He opens his mouth to argue the point, but then notices the angle of light slanting through the trees, checks the time on his phone. Nearly three o'clock.

"Sorry about that," feeling sheepish before this young and serious woman. "I guess I…." But he doesn't know how to explain to her how he lost two hours without a trace.

"Well, I guess there's no use crying about it now." From the bed of her truck, Catherine pulls out a large hiking pack and laces her arms through the straps. "Best make use of what time we have left." Barely checking to make sure he's following, she walks to the trailhead and into the forest's mouth.

THE PATH RIDES UP and over a shoulder of roots and stone, then immediately drops down the western slope of whatever foothill or mountain they might be on, and through the trees Ben can see the intermittent twinkling jewel of Lake Tahoe, the clear cool swath of sky, the vague and brilliant smear of sun, and with Catherine a steady receding point ahead of him, Ben becomes aware all at once—in the pulse of his skull, the sour flop of his belly—of his recent days of drinking, of stumbling lost through the desert and through the city, of sleeping on Alex's couch. His spine feels like a crippled branch about to break. His head is a dirty fishbowl. He sees Catherine's canteen swaying from her backpack and wishes she'd offer him a drink. He knows she never will. A girl who fears him or hates him but takes him anyway into her

TO SLEEP AS ANIMALS

mountains and trees. A steady receding point leading him into the wild.

She will abandon me here, he decides, if I allow her to. So he speaks to her to slow her down.

"Is there a specific," and he pants, "grove or something where you know these Indian pipes grow?"

"Not in any one place in particular." She isn't slowing down. "They grow all up and down throughout the valley. Sometimes completely underground."

"Underground?"

"They don't photosynthesize, so they don't need light."

For a moment, the whole scene flickers: how can something live without light?

"I was under the impression"—impressed, impressed upon—"that they only grew"—imposed upon, disposed of—"near the water."

"The territory *Sarcodes sanguinea* cover is pretty expansive, Dr. Nigra." And for a moment it seems like she might look over her shoulder at him. "From high arid altitudes to marshy lowlands." But she's only turning to watch a bird glide among pine and fir. "A very adaptable species."

"I think you might be confusing," he says, "your ambitions for my own." Ben loses sight of the bird before he's sure he's even seen it. "It's Mr. Nigra. Not doctor."

The soft thump of feet on earth. The creak of old limbs. Dropping needles and the faint swish of moving air. Silence.

"If the species is so adaptable," Ben eventually asks, "why is it found only around this one lake? Why isn't it all over the place?"

And finally Catherine does stop, rolling her shoulders within the straps of her pack and leaning against a tree. Instead of twin braids, today she wears a single ponytail, which she lifts to peel off her sweaty neck and drops again over one shoulder.

"There's something about this place," she says, "that allows certain things—strong things, even—to survive here but nowhere else. Even gentler environments will kill them. These Indian pipes can survive drought and blizzard and flooding, all within a single year, but in the stasis of the lab, I have yet to get one sample to survive." And she sighs. "There's a dependency with this landscape that I don't understand."

This, Ben realizes, is the true crux of her dilemma. Not to prove a suspected truth but to develop a new method for understanding this thing that cannot now be understood. This is what he was hoping for, seeking out. It's something he can understand. How do you examine the nature of a thing if the granted tools unilaterally destroy the subject of your curiosity? How do you adapt without becoming dependent? How do you prove what refuses to be proved? He knows enough not to say any of this.

"I hope you can figure out," he says, "what makes this place so unique."

Unclipping her canteen from her pack, she thanks him with a tired smile, and when he asks her for a drink, she surprises him by handing him her water.

YET LIKE A FILM reel burning up under the projector's hot glare, Ben watches this moment of fleeting alliance—this truce of water—flicker out, the timeline peeling frame by frame, scenes dithering and melting together. Ben follows the path Catherine guides him along and is lost but willing to follow, and when later she leaves him and he's alone—the word, he reminds himself, is *abandoned*—he follows the path gravity dictates and is certain he knows the way. Even as he draws further away. Even when the trail is gone. Stumbling blind and sliding, forgetting where he is: Ben follows any path he finds himself centered on.

When Ben met Ethyl, he was blinded by the dark and she saw that he was blind, could see him not seeing. After walking the floor of the Peppermill—with its laser-tag carpet and bright gold machines belching coins and spinning casters—Ben stepped into the first lounge he found, a long black place lit only by thin lines of violet neon, not so much illuminating as accentuating the interior dusk. He ordered a double Scotch on the rocks. Blinked his eyes to adjust to the darkness. Felt his eyes not adjusting. Leaned on the bar beside Ethyl but was unaware of her blank shape impressed against the concealing purple light. When his drink came and he paid, Ben carefully stepped toward a corner booth and was about to slide onto the bench when he realized the table was already occupied. Two sets of staring eyes, barely gleaming reflected neon and gauging him in the dark. He smiled an unseen apology and moved to another table. But again: that faint gloss of purple light shining off ungiving eyes, a lone figure with a glass in his hands gazing up at Ben's interrupting shape. As if every seemingly empty space contained something that did not want him. He mumbled apology and moved back to the bar, back to the spot where he had just been, and when he settled on the stool and looked down into his glass, Ethyl spoke up beside him as if they'd already been speaking, were in the middle of a conversation whose thread had been interrupted but now, at last, could be resumed.

"I once took a Nigerian man as a lover," she said, her voice both ragged but somehow silky, a practiced rough sensuality. "He'd spent most of his life in this country, growing up and going to school and doing the customary American thing. Worked a decent job, got married once and then divorced, finally made up his mind never to make that mistake again. Outright owned his house and car and had a nice dog and so was American. But still, he'd grown up in Africa, in Nigeria, so was Nigerian, too. He spent his first seven or eight years in Nigeria, running around bare-bellied and going to school in the basement of the local church because it was the biggest space and was cool in the summer. And then at some point the Biafran Revolution happened, and he and his family became Biafrans, and then almost immediately became refugees without a country. That's when they came to the United States. That's when he became an American."

She looked at him while she spoke. But to Ben, she was just a solid black shape embossing the barroom's vaporous black. In the pauses between words, she'd turn away, look at the bottles all lined up between them and the functionless backdrop mirror. A ridge of brow. A purse of lips. An incline of nose between. The suggestion of identity yet with nothing tangible to hold onto. Sometimes he could see the lashes of her eyes. Sometimes he could see the creases around her mouth. Ben sipped his drink and watched her, saying nothing.

"Seeing you just now," she went on, "shuffling between these tables, not even seeing the people

TO SLEEP AS ANIMALS

around you, it made me think of something my Nigerian man once told me. About this ritual that his people once did. Not all of them, mind you. The part of Nigeria that became Biafra was a mix of Westernized urban intellectuals and I guess what you'd call traditional natives, okay, so in situations like that, there's always people on one side who think they're *above* whatever folks on the other side do. But the religious and traditional types took part in this thing where they'd assemble a mask out of many small pieces, out of other masks—this was their ritual—and they'd assemble this mask around one person. And when they were done, this thing would be over seven feet tall, all huge and covered in the faces of all these different masks that were now really just one big mask, you know, surrounding his whole body, and the poor man inside would become possessed by the mask. In the eyes of these people, there wasn't even a person inside the mask anymore. There would just be the mask, and the body inside would be its skeleton."

Ben imagined a black shaggy heap of bone and hair and wailing faces carved of aged-brown wood. He imagined the Viking monster behind the diner's grill.

"When the mask was completed and the guy inside was fully possessed, pregnant women and children weren't allowed to look at it. The mask contained a great evil. Who knows what would happen if such weak and impressionable people laid eyes on it! That's why they disassembled it when it wasn't in use. The evil had to be dismantled and scattered."

She stopped to drain the fluid from her glass, and without saying anything or even looking up, Ben gestured and the bartender appeared with a fresh drink, removing the spent glass and installing a new one between Ethyl's hands. The faint toothy gloss of her smile in the non-light: Ethyl took another sip before continuing.

"I can't remember what the point of this masking ritual was or maybe my Nigerian friend never told me. But I remember *when* he told me. It was the first time we had slept together. I had danced for him plenty of times—he would come into the club and request me, had me do private dances for him until my shift ended, but later he'd just buy me drinks and talk to me. Like my job was to be good company, not necessarily to dance. And anyway, we'd gone on a few dates, too, but they were always so cordial, almost like high school. He was so polite. And finally one night, we made love. I'd taken him to a hot spring up in the foothills and it was a bright night with a fat moon and we made love in the steaming water. It was January, so with the cold air and the hot water, the whole thing was…over*whelm*ing. The way we were wrapped up in each other and we'd dunk and splash…. But afterward when we were just lying there up to our chins soaking, he grew quiet. Not distant. Just quiet. And then he told me about this mask. This mask full of evil that swallowed its wearer whole.

"And I remember him clearly saying that the mask did not cast a shadow and that the man in the mask did not cast a shadow. Their shadows, he said, were trapped inside a magic mirror. Until the mask released the man inside, his shadow would remain in the mirror."

Ben finished his drink. Ethyl gestured for him. The bartender brought another. Faintly music played and even fainter, through the walls, Ben could hear the sounds of the surrounding casino.

Voices and change rattling and laughter reflecting. Everything so muffled and far away inside the insular dark of the lounge.

"You watched me fumbling for a seat," he finally said, "and it reminded you of your friend and his story of a mask."

"That's right."

"Why?"

And she laughed at him. "Do you see your shadow in here?" And she stroked a hand down the length of his back, and this time more kindly said, "Do you see mine?"

Beyond the dark and black light neon: golden doorways leading back to the casino floor, so bright as to mean nearly nothing, all detail and distinction erased in the uninterrupted reveal of light.

"Why would anyone," he smiled, knowing she could not see it, "build a mask like that around himself?"

And again, this indistinct figure laughed through the vaporous dark.

"Like you don't know."

And as Ben wanders down this Tahoe mountainside—as the day slips by in long-lashed strands of light between the trees, as the muscles in his legs burn into a rubbery numbness, as he finds the red alien upshoot of the Indian pipe jetting out from a fist of roots—he again and again covers his face with the living veil of his hand. Hiding his eyes or peering between fingers yet still, never seeing. Even as Catherine, warmed up to him now, walks alongside him chattering. Even as Catherine disappears ahead of him on the path and is gone. The Ponderosas swallow him like krill into baleen and hours later filter him out, not at the peak where his Jeep is parked on the ruts and moss off Route 50 but at the base of the mountain, at the edge of the lake and Tahoe's minor outskirts. It's grown dark: the streetlights he walks under turn his shadow into something monstrous. Nothing man-like. Not even *his* shadow. The shadow of a dog scurrying at his feet. A mask made of masks. A mirror full of shadows. Against the sky: the silhouette of a gondola riding up the mountainside. Ben walks toward town and into the first large structure he finds, a lakeside casino whose name he forgets or never learns, and in dirty clothes and with a bit-through bloody lip, he drinks free beer while playing the slots until he finds someone willing to drive him up the mountain to his Jeep, and finally he can go home.

Chapter 7

When Ben was a boy and saw the sun as something small and weak then saw its blinding might—when he surrendered to gravity and the summer-swollen belly of the creek's winding flow—he emerged soaked and quiet and peacefully somnambulant, walking through the brush and forest in a meditative calm, and even when he walked from the woods into his backyard up toward his house and his mom saw him—ran rushing from where she'd been hanging damp clothes on the line to kneel and scoop him off his feet, to hold him in the grass in the warm puzzle of her arms, asking what happened, where he'd been, what happened—his calm would not unknot. He saw and could feel how his mom was concerned but could not understand why she should be. He was gone and now was back and wet with a river's tongue. How could something so simple mean anything? He let her hold him because it seemed important to her. But he did not tell her where he'd been.

A snuffling nuzzle. A wet mouth on his eyes and cheek. Finally, his mom peeled off his clothes and rung the river's breath from them, hung them to sun-dry with the others on the line, led him naked through the yard into the house's dark robes.

BACK AT THE MOTEL, Ben sloughs off his soiled clothes and runs the shower, hunkers in the tub in an achy daze, slipping in and out of shallow naps until the hot water runs out and he has to briskly wash himself in the biting pinprick cold. He shaves taking care around the swollen split lip he doesn't yet remember biting through. Barefoot and shirtless, he buys a bottle of the cheapest vodka the Quikie Mart offers, cleans the rough cut over the bathroom sink.

At the front desk, there is another letter waiting, its stamp obscured by a Syracuse postmark. Back in his room, he opens the envelope, but inside is only a single square of white cardstock. On one side it reads, in thick block letters,

> **NOSTOS**

On the other side:

> **ALGOS**

He crumples the letter and throws it in the trash. He takes his camera into the bathroom and takes a picture of his mouth in the mirror. Stares at his face in the glass until he no longer recognizes who it is he sees, what mask stares stolidly back. He doesn't want to be in this room anymore.

Because everything else is dirty and maybe ruined, Ben dresses in Dickies and a T-shirt. Because he sees him haunting the Quikie Mart sidewalk, Ben picks up Earl and takes him along through town to the Peppermill. "You drink on me tonight, friend." Earl beams like a child as the city lights pass so fast overhead, all around.

In the otherwise empty lounge, they find Ethyl at the bar and join her, buy her a drink, laugh in the neon-streaking gloom and soon enough befriend an off-duty taxi driver named Carl with the pale brows and nose of a retired pugilist but the body of a river stone: round and flat. His voice is a rope and his laugh a harpoon. "I spent most of my life somewhere else altogether," he says, "fucking whatever girls I could, scraping my brains off the ceiling most nights, and shit, hoss, I hated almost every second of it and never once thought about leaving. Cocaine and Cuban sleaze-bags every day of my life. I watched the sun set in the Gulf and watched the sun rise from the Atlantic's fat guts and it all seemed like some sick

To Sleep as Animals

twisted Beach Boys heroin dream, you know? Then for almost no reason whatsoever I saved some money and flew to San Francisco for a weekend. I didn't fucking once leave my fucking motel room. I killed the mini-bar and watched television. I could have been anywhere. I couldn't wait to go home. But then on my flight back, I got trapped here. My plane was grounded, everywhere else in the world was a blizzard. I hung around casinos and talked to the pimps on the street and you know, I developed a genuine affection for this place. I cashed in what I could of my ticket and I ain't ever left since. And I still fuck whoever will grace me with her cunt. I still scrape my brains off the walls. If I were a prince, this'd be my fucking kingdom." He drains the last foamy swallow from the bottom of his bottle and sets it on the counter so that it spins a dangerous turn. "But enough about me, hoss. How'd you end up in this skid mark of a city?"

If there were other people in the lounge when they arrived, they're all long gone by now.

"What, no, I'm here on business," and Ben grins a whiskey grin, wide enough to reopen his split lip. "I'm a researcher." A black slip of blood drips down his chin.

"Researching what?"

He jerks a thumb at Ethyl. "Whatever she's already found."

But whatever he was hoping to gain by this is lost: she isn't paying attention.

"You know these are free," the bartender reminds them whenever he brings another round, "out there, right?" pointing out the door at the casino at large.

"I used to bring in over half a million dollars each year," Earl tells them. "After taxes. I barely did a thing. I showed up at work and told people what to do and what I told them earned our firm ridiculous amounts of money. I couldn't sneeze without making money. I could have been making much more." He pours a splash from Ethyl's glass into his own, sloshes the liquid around, swallows it ice and all. "Doesn't even seem like something I ever did. Seems like someone else's life."

"You've only ever lived this one life," Ethyl corrects him. "No one ever gets to live more than one. Just about everyone is proof of that."

The bartender tries to hide in the shadows between the ultraviolet lights. Out somewhere in the casino, a man loses everything and wails.

"Back in those days when I was first sticking around here," Carl says, "I knew this guy who was cursed. It was something hereditary. His pop and both brothers had it and probably all his uncles, too, everyone, all the men in his family, they all had it and so did my friend, though he did everything he could to get away from it."

The alcohol blows a cool breeze through Ben's skull, down his neck, through his skin and into his body. On his one side, Carl pulls a long draw from his bottle of unlimed Pacifico. On his one side, Earl leans in to put his arm around Ethyl and kiss her softly on the cheek. "You're over-generous, dear," he whispers, and her ripped-open laugh rises like a siren through the lounge.

"How'd your ear get so small, child?"

"It's stupid, it's a bad movie. You wouldn't believe me if I told you."

"Try me."

And Earl nestles into her sweet smelling neck and hair. "When I was a kid I got hit by a train."

"Good god!"

Ben cannot feel his eyes. He closes his eyes and everything looks exactly the same.

"Yeah. Our car was parked on the tracks. When the train hit, my dad smashed the door open with the force of it and flew out and I flew out after him and somehow before my mom came flying through too, the door swung shut again so she had to plow it open just like my dad. I was tossed clear of the wreck but they both died. On account of that door being shut both times."

He imagines bright light screaming through the darkness, swelling and expanding and deafeningly loud until there is no dark and there is no sound, just that monstrous flooding light. Erasing every distinct thing in a wash of purifying white.

"And that's when your ear got small?"

"Sort of. I had to walk six miles to find some help. The first house I came to, some dog attacked me. Bit off most of my left ear. Just kind of hopped up and nipped it right off." Ben opens his eyes and Earl's grinning into the dark. "Guess they never fed him. His owners, I mean."

Beside him, Ethyl holds his head under her chin and coos, softly strokes his filthy hair while Earl, happy and mellow with breasts against his face, calmly stirs his drink with a finger. "I told you you wouldn't believe me."

"Tough break, hoss," and Carl finishes his beer with a glug and vibrant belch.

Meanwhile, three women in heels and little else have come into the lounge, walked in cackling and loud but now stand framed in the doorway watching the four of them at the bar. A barfly and bum and their bleary-eyed escorts. The women turn on unsteady feet and leave before they've ever really arrived. Carl salutes them as they go and orders another round.

"I almost bit off my lip today."

"What'd you do that for?"

"Couldn't tell you."

Carl raspberries and shakes his head. "Lame." Beside them, Ethyl and Earl are all just lips and tongues, soft moans, are making out. "My cursed friend use to work at one of the nuclear test sites around here. Some kind of meter reader, I guess. Walking around the desert in a spacesuit after each blast, following a Geiger counter like it was one of those sticks people use to find water. Probably just as pointless, too, when you consider what he was looking for. But hey, he felt fulfilled by this. He thought he was saving himself from this curse he had."

"Which was what?"

"Huh?"

"What was the family curse?"

"To die in a kitchen."

The bartender's ignoring them now. Ben has to shout to finally get a drink.

"Lived out at the test site's dormitory, ate at the cafeteria or occasionally in town at some shitty restaurant. Never had to use a kitchen, not once. But then he got caught sabotaging some equipment at the test site and they sent him to federal prison for ten years. Worked in the laundry. Ate in the mess hall. His thirties came and went and he never saw one kitchen."

"Why'd he sabotage the equipment?"

"Had a change of heart, I guess. I think it had something to do with Indians, but I don't know, I never really thought of him as one. But they take that shit personally, you know, lighting off atomic bombs over their ancestral fucking home or whatever."

"The last time I was in a prison," Ethyl chimes in, detaching herself from Earl's arms and mouth, "it was a conjugal visit. One of my suitors had gotten himself caught driving stolen cars between chop shops and got put away for three years. He and I weren't married, but I knew he had a wife that had run off a long time ago to somewhere up in Utah. No one had seen her in years. So I pretended I was her. Just imagine his surprise to be moping around the prison yard feeling like a severe detriment to his own life, and then some guard comes up and tells him his estranged wife who he hasn't seen in years is there to see him on a conjugal visit. Now imagine his surprise when he steps into the trailer and finds me there instead."

"You did that for three years?"

"Until I got bored." And she returns to the cool comfort of her drink. "Until he started expecting me to come."

For a second, Ben thinks that this might have been her Nigerian man. He knows it probably was not her Nigerian man, but still: he hopes it might have been. Wants to ask if it was. If only to bring the conversation back to him. To his short life in another country. To his people, men of faith. Evil spirits and trapping mirrors. To watch your country disappear because another country wants it more or anyway, doesn't want *you* to have it: how do you forgive something like that? He tries to ask her about these things but someone interrupts him before he's even begun, says something indistinct that erupts laughter from everyone and Ben forgets what he meant to ask, tries to take a drink but finds his glass empty again and when the bartender ignores his request for more, Ben goes behind the counter, fixes everyone another of whatever they're each drinking. But before he's had a sip of his own, two men like boulders in sharp clean suits appear in the lounge and ask them all to leave.

"You can stay, of course," they say to Ethyl, and the bartender agrees, "if you want."

"Of course, darling, thank you." She doesn't even watch them go as the three men are led out through the casino and into the night air outside, and with nowhere to go and nothing in particular to do, they pile into Ben's Jeep and drive, windows down and Earl in the back bemoaning his near brush with and sudden loss of rare female affection. Dark bedroom windows and empty dead-grass lawns. Casino promenades and lights

To Sleep as Animals

muted by a thin skin of dust. Since he's been here, Ben hasn't seen it rain once.

Near the 777 they see Zack and two other grey men milling about half-drunk and blathering on the sidewalk. Ben pulls to the curb and invites them for a ride.

"C'mon in, brothers," he shouts. "We'll abscond from the highway into the desert night. We'll hunt quail with our headlights."

Two of the men pile in back but Zack remains on the street. "No way, man. I can see the exact trouble you're aiming for." But he's smiling, friendly and kind. "I'm keeping my *feet* on the ground." They leave him standing outside the 777 and head to the strip clubs south of town.

"I fell in love tonight," Earl announces, "and was betrayed for the easy vanity of a familiar bouncer who remembered her name."

The grey men coo their support. Up front, Carl shakes his head and searches the radio for a station playing the game—any game—but fails and quits, leaves the dial somewhere between stations. James Brown and 80s dance music bleed together as one, fills the silence with something dizzyingly passionate and shallow, and before they reach the clubs Ben decides his buzz is running too thin. At a drive-thru liquor store, Ben buys a pint of Old Crow from the cigarette-thin woman working behind the window and hands the bottle to Carl as he pulls back out onto the street. Carl cracks the seal and they pass the pint of Old Crow as they ride. Around them, Madonna and Aretha try and fail to say the same exact thing.

But of course, the clubs won't take them in. Three of them homeless and all of them drunk. No one will take them in. So they park by the loading dock behind one club and watch the dancers come and go on their cigarette breaks between sets.

"This is villainy," Earl cries from the back. "The classist bigotry of a fascist regime. This is why I quit the white-collar life of shuffling decimal points and breeding dollar signs. This is why I cashed in and pulled out."

"What," Carl turns a skeptical eye to the grey man, "so you could get turned away from tittie bars?"

"Because unless you're suffering with the slime on bottom, you're part of the scum up top."

"Cheers to that," and Ben passes the bottle to the back.

"When my friend got out of jail," Carl goes on, "the whole lot of us threw a party for him. A bunch of old friends, you know, but mostly lady relatives. Sisters and aunts and young cousins with pretty eyes and freckles. Not an uncle or nephew in sight.

"Anyway, the party was at his older sister's house, right, out in the hills north of here. Fucking *nice* country up there in the night with her house all lit up like a candle and this guy and his family burning all bright inside. It was like a fucking wedding the way everyone smiled and laughed and cried all at once. Like he was a bride about to marry his freedom.

"So sure, they were all pretty happy to have their boy back. But mostly they were celebrating because they thought the curse had been lifted. All the other men in the family had died before their thirty-third birthday. One of them—an uncle, I guess, who my friend never had a chance to meet—didn't make it past five. Fell out of the sink when his mom was giving him a bath. Broke his neck on the floor. Most of them got a little longer go at it than that, but still. They all died before middle age. And here's this guy at forty and not having even seen a kitchen for ten years. He'd beat the curse! Everyone was certain he'd beat it."

Across the lot at the back of the club, the women in their hip-length robes tiptoe back inside, slip back out, returning to the strut and bounce of the stage or returning to the outer dark where the air is cool and almost unmoving beneath the unfurling night bloom of sky.

"He spent most of the night drinking right there in his sister's kitchen. Leaning against the fridge or sitting at this table that looked like a dog had chewed it all to hell. Sitting like he belonged there among all the knives and glasses and the coils on the stove. Like he fit right in there."

In the back, one of the grey men begins making choked gurgling sounds. Earl helps force the man's head and shoulders out the passenger-side rear window. The women behind the club are watching, pulled from their communal rite of aloneness, exhale smoke and watch. Ben guns the engine and gets them out of there.

WAGONEER RIPPING throatily from the strip club's back lot and onto a vacant side-street—gasping grey man puking out the window—Earl makes clear his sudden unwavering desire to place a bet on a horse. On a specific horse in a specific race. One that is about to begin. "I've got an inside line," he says, touching the ragged scar-line of his ear. "I'm a prophet where money flows." Though it all sounds to Ben like grandiose inebriate fantasy, he agrees to Earl's request and with Carl as his navigator, finds a discrete bookmaker's shop, a basement betting parlor nested in the back of an old brick building on the outskirts of the downtown, a pressed-tin sign riveted to the mortar above the stairs leading down.

"They won't let me in here," Earl says, digging in his jacket. "You have to place this for me." And he hands Ben a wad of bills.

Ben doesn't bother asking where this money came from. He leaves them all behind in his Jeep and trots down the stairs into the basement betting parlor.

Inside, there are stuffed chairs arranged around tables with dirty ashtrays, TVs mounted in the corners near the ceiling, and even though the man taking bets is inside a bulletproof cage, there's the feeling of a 1950s living room. Wainscoting and empty bookshelves and pictures on the walls and, almost as an afterthought, a young man parked in the dimness of one corner between the outside wall and the bulletproof cage, in shirt sleeves and shoulder holster and some ridiculous interpretation of a Stetson. Skeptical, Ben approaches the cage and asks about the next race and when it turns out to be the one Earl had anticipated—some vague event, in Japan of all places—Ben puts all the money on a horse named Sparkleberry. Yet it's only as the bookmaker counts out the bills that Ben realizes the wad is made entirely of twenties and fifties. A bum's dirty grand riding on a Japanese horse.

There are only two other men in the basement parlor, an old man in an oversized jacket and loose flapping slacks, and a younger man in a brown suit with matching mustache and thinning frizzy hair. Ben takes his ticket and sits at the old man's table, says an unrequited hello, waits for the race to begin on the TV.

Across the parlor, the mustached man watches Ben with a persistent needling glower. Ben shapes his face into a mask of insolence and turns away, picks up an abandoned newspaper, starts reading about protesters at the Yucca nuclear facility getting beaten by the police. The dateline, he notices, is August 4th, 2003. July is days past and gone. He arrived here in July and now July is gone. The surprise of this waxes and wanes and when the old man beside him says something vague and derogatory, Ben looks up—first at the man, then the TV—and realizes he's missed the race. He missed the race he came to see and Sparkleberry won. The horse Earl bet on won.

"Hey," he says, "my horse won."

The old man's lips peel around a mouthful of dentures. "Good for you."

"I've never done this before. What am I supposed to do?"

"Take your ticket to the window. Frank will do the rest."

So Ben takes the ticket to the bulletproof cage and as the bookmaker counts out the stacks of bills, Ben grins and taps his fingers on the counter, dances in place, surprises himself by being excited about the win even if it isn't his own. But gradually he becomes aware of a presence at his elbow and a voice like an insect's whine—the buzz of a broken machine—and with a flash of recognition Ben turns to the brown-suited man at his side.

"You can't do that."

"Excuse me?"

"You think you can do this?"

"Yeah."

"You can't. You think you can waltz in without any idea of what you're doing and win everything and then just walk away. But there are rules."

"It's Joel, right?"

"Huh?" The man's whole body seems to stutter. "What?"

"You're name is Joel. You ditched me at the airport last week."

Inside his cage, the bookmaker says something about letting it go, there's nothing personal about the game. In his corner, the young holstered man slowly stands at attention. But the brown man keeps at it—"You can't walk in and take everything like that, you can't!"—his mustache twitching like some living thing strapped to his lip, and when the money passes through the window into Ben's hands, the brown man makes a leap for it.

"It's not fair!"

With one hand, Ben catches the man's face and pushes him to the floor. He goes down like a sandcastle, like a domino, something designed to fall. Ben stuffs the money into the pockets of his pants and when the man stands up again, Ben grabs him by his collar and forces him to the floor, crouches over him like a spider over a fly.

Cutting through the light pouring down on them, the shadow of the Stetsoned man splashes across their bodies and onto the floor and freezes. The unmistakable sound of a pistol drawn and cocked. He'd recognize that silhouette anywhere: it brings Ben some comfort to know that someone somewhere feels it necessary to aim a weapon at his back. It's like, for the first time in weeks, he's actually doing his job.

Leaning low over the prostrate man, Ben breathes huskily in his face:

"You're a weasel, Joel, and you're skulking outside my back door. You left me in the lurch once before. Now you cry when I win something that was never meant to be yours. If you don't like losing, Joel, you should stay out of the fucking game. You cannot be weak and still win. If I catch you in my roost again, I'll string your guts from the rafters."

And in this moment, crouching over this quivering wreck of a human, he believes it. He's certain he'll kill this man. Him or someone like him.

Taking his winnings, Ben measures his stride by the scope of his breath and steps out from the basement parlor into the city night air. He sees his friends inside his Jeep and feels a balloon burst of pride. His slouching Wagoneer with a grey streak of vomit spraying along one fender. His ruined liberated men whose minds are maps and whose skin has been burned by the sun and burned by the night. This is their city. These streets belong to them.

Back in the driver's seat, Ben leans over the console and dumps the money into Earl's lap. A shocked silence floods the cab, followed by a thunderclap of laughter.

"Holy shit!" Carl's twisted sideways in his seat, eyes wide and hungry as he gapes at the grey man's easy win. "There's something like a grand there."

The grey men are a hooting delirious chorus, hysterical and incoherent. Ben guns the engine and surges into the street.

The air pouring in the windows is thicker now and charred. Like mosquitoes drawing close, shying away: sirens come and go, screaming all around. But whatever emergency that's happening is far away, has nothing to do with them. They cruise a few blocks and jet through a red light but then stop at the next, and craning his neck to see Earl, Ben asks how he knew to bet right then on that particular horse. But somehow the words sound different as they pour out of his mouth. All wrong. Asking something else all together.

"How come your parents were parked on the railroad tracks, Earl?"

And now no one is hooting or hysterical. Now no one breathes a sound.

From the moment they raced away from the betting parlor, Earl has been peeling off the red paper bands holding his stacks of bills neatly together, turning his orderly bricks into a chaos of loose paper. With Ben's question still hanging in the air, Earl looks up from his work and stares Ben in the eyes. Makes a humorless shape of his mouth like a grin, some sort of laughing sound with his nose. Tries not to show his teeth. But neither he nor Ben says a word.

The other two grey men watch horrified and uncertain. Carl stares into his lap, shaking his head, waiting. When the light turns green, he nudges Ben and they continue down the avenue, unaware of any destination, just moving to be anywhere but here.

After a while, Earl begins dictating turns, trades places with the grey man seated behind Carl, and when they pass through a worn-down neighborhood—derelict vehicles slouched in the driveways, hand-me-down toys scattered in brown lawns—Earl leans out his open window and throws handfuls of loose bills into the night. He shouts something victorious but the meaning is lost to the wind or his throat or maybe was never there as the money flies from his hands into the dead grass, into the gutters, along the sidewalk and in the street.

"Jesus Christ," Carl shouts, "what'd you do that for?"

Earl slips back inside the Jeep, eyes bright and cheeks wind-chapped red. "Wealth redistribution, my friend. We're stealing from the rich and giving to the poor."

"Who the fuck are you, Walt Whitman?"

They continue surveying the rundown neighborhoods, dollar bills fluttering in the wake until Earl feels he's left with a reasonable nest egg, at which point his damaged libido comes creeping back to the forefront of his mind. He demands a prostitute and the other grey men agree, they want a prostitute for Earl, a slew of them. So Ben cruises the darker, more haunted streets. Past empty storefronts and the occasional car idling in the shadows between street lamps. When Earl tells him to stop near a clutch of tall bony women gathered in the shadowed recess of a boarded-up drugstore doorway, Ben pulls to the curb and the three grey men pile out.

He watches them approach the pack and introduce themselves. Watches Earl step forward as their leader. Watches his mouth silently twist words in the air. Inside the Jeep, all he can hear is Sam Cooke's passionate croon, ambushed by wavering synths and bubbly cartoon drums. Carl sucks his teeth in disgust. "We should *not* be here." Women in shadows, hairy arms and Adam's apples. Ben watches as Earl touches tenderly the cheek of the closest dark-eyed whore, can almost feel the rasp against his fingertips.

He's aware, watching this, of a small part of him dying. The longing in Earl's touch, his eyes. It hurts to see such want and delusion. "He wants so bad to be with a woman," he says, "but his company will always be with men."

He shifts the Jeep into drive. He quickly pulls away from the curb.

"Good call," Carl says, even as Earl jerks at the engine's sound, "Best idea you've had all night," even as Earl starts running after them. His shouts barely audible. Just revving and the radio's sad amalgam of song. Spinning the wheel, Ben tries to pull a U-turn but realizes too late that a low concrete median divides the opposing lane. "Fuck fuck *fuck*." The Jeep rises like a rearing horse, bucks and drops heavily in the other lane with a sickening metal crunch, and as Ben tries to regain control, right his trajectory and escape up the street, suddenly Earl is standing on the yellow middle line, arms wide like a goaltender and a look on his face like some mistake has been made, someone misunderstood, this can all be fixed.

Ben tries to swerve. Carl is laughing but stops with the thump of impact.

And for one horrible second, Earl is there beside him, hanging desperately from the sideview mirror and shouting, trying to bang on the closed window—"It's a mistake, Ben, it's okay"—before the Jeep hits a pothole and the grey man drops off and is gone.

"Jesus."

"Huh?"

They travel a long time without speaking. The radio sizzles and fries and eventually Ben snaps it off. There are police cruisers in the streets but they're fast and flashing and off on other business. Carl silently works his mouth and lips as if they're new and don't fit well. Whenever Ben pushes the accelerator, the Jeep's engine grates and whines. Like a wounded animal forced to pull a load. He becomes aware of the faint stink of dirty bodies permeating the cab. He rolls down all the windows to blow the stink out into the night.

Douglas W. Milliken

This is what Ben remembers of the mountain:

He remembers meeting Catherine and feeling tired and hungover, not sure why he was there with her outside Tahoe and not sure how he had lost like loose change two hours on the road;

He remembers Catherine's anger and the fear hiding beneath her anger's shallow skin;

He remembers in his mind blaming the hitchhiker for the missing time, conscious of no evidence to back-up his blame, blamed the hitchhiker nevertheless;

He remembers wishing he were better at living, under Catherine's narrow eyes wished he didn't have to pretend, that he could genuinely identify with the needs and wants and motives of the people surrounding him;

He remembers the grade being steep;

And the quality of the light, sharp and surreal between the skewering blades of the trees;

And the needles on the rocks turning slick beneath his feet;

And Catherine's ponytail bobbing like a carrot on a stick, leading him toward something vague and maybe not wanted, and he remembers that when she paused in the trail and spoke to him finally as if he were actually there—spoke openly to him about her project and its pitfalls—for one fleeting second he understood how she felt, did not have to guess or imagine but knew, really knew because he recognized himself in her, recognized the possible futility of seeking out something that might be just out of reach, and in realizing this realized too why she was so scared of him, her fear masked in anger, realized he threatened her by being like her, that she too saw herself in him and it terrified her to know that she could be older and weaker, more damaged and more lost and still unwilling to quit, running herself into the ground trying repeatedly to obtain what she could never obtain;

He remembers thinking of Ethyl just then, and her contempt for all the girls dancing in the footlights;

He remembers, for one moment, thinking of his cousin;

The daylight was downshifting and the air was cooling and Ben remembers feeling at ease with Catherine, remembers Catherine feeling finally at ease with him, as if somehow in seeing one another in the mirror of themselves there was no need now for fear or defense, but he does not remember when or how their conversation soured and he does not remember how things so abruptly changed;

He remembers standing dizzy and nauseous in the trail and not recognizing the slope and bend of the path ahead or behind, knowing something had come and gone and he lost it and did not know what he'd lost;

He remembers feeling the bitter chalk of Hanover's name in his mouth but cannot recall how the geochemist fit into what they'd been talking about;

He remembers calling out Catherine's name;

He remembers watching her run;

And then for a long time, there was nothing to remember: he stood in the trail, he counted his breaths, he waited for the nausea to pass;

Squirrels scurried around him in the path;

Squirrels scurried away;

He does not remember chewing his lip, biting finally through the soft meat, ripped and bleeding and still being chewed;

He remembers thinking about his cousin;

He remembers laying his hand over his face;

Ben remembers thinking about his cousin;

But then he heard someone sneeze nearby, invisible and beyond the bend of the trail or in the woods surrounding, and he thought it might be Catherine but it could be anyone, he wanted it to be anyone, in that moment he remembers needing someone to save him;

He remembers his paralysis breaking as he searched up and down the trail for someone to find, remembers diving off the path into the dense shade of the woods;

He remembers spinning around searching and the long splintered light through the pines tapping a hammer to a spot behind his eyes, inside his skull, and he remembers sneezing, head shaking like a dog, and he remembers realizing a moment later how all this silly flailing through the woods began;

He remembers feeling like a fool;

He remembers not caring that he's always been a fool;

But once in the woods, he decided he preferred being away from the confines of the trail, and in turn decided he would continue and find the snow plant on his own, he could find it alone, in fact would have better luck out here, away from the trail, far from any path trapping him to its middle;

He remembers believing he was choosing his own way among the Ponderosas, guiding himself by memory and logic and the things he thought he saw but did not really see, believed he was in control even as gravity's leash dragged him perpetually downhill, always further down the mountain, even when he thought he was climbing up, he was not;

He remembers wandering and searching and once leaning in a crouch against a root-rotted tree pitching with the grade, eyes closed and breathing slow as the day's light crept further away from him, but mostly he does not remember much because there was not much to remember, stumbling and seeking and finding nothing, and also because his mind was on other things—on being blackly trapped in a Nigerian mask, on the possibility of being fatally lost so far away from anyone or anything he could honestly say he knew or understood, on his cousin and the facts about himself and her that he will eventually have to face—and also, too, above all else, Ben cannot remember what he did alone for hours lost on a mountain because he was asleep, was sleepwalking in defense against his mind and its spinning fear;

Ben can't remember because he wasn't really there;

Ben cannot know what his body was doing when his mind had so long ago punched out;

So Ben remembers a dream where he was lost and searching blindly for something he did not really care to find;

He remembers wanting desperately for it anyway to be found.

"SO WHAT HAPPENED to your friend?" he finally asks. Outside, the city passes in a slow sterile strobe. "The one who had the curse."

The wind whipping in smells like a chimney: creosote and smoke.

"He died." Carl stares ahead, unblinking, unseeing. His voice is a low tired thing. "Got stabbed to death in his sister's kitchen."

"Who stabbed him?"

"Some Mexican kids. No one really knew them. They kind of just invited themselves in. For the most part, no one minded them, but one of the kids, this one pretty boy, he got jealous that none of the girls were paying any attention to him, that they were all fawning over the man of the hour. The kid had no idea what was going on. So he walked up to my friend and started talking shit, the sort of macho jab that is supposed to cut someone else down while boosting yourself up. But you know, my friend had just spent ten years in jail. He'd seen his fair share of shit-talking punks and knew how to put them in their place. Made some sort of comment about the kid's sculpted hair, his dark eye lashes, you know, pretty much calling him out as a faggot in front of all his friends and all these pretty girls. Needless to say, the kid didn't dig it.

"So, you know, the pretty boy and his friends took off. And the party was quiet for a while but after a minute or two, everything was fine. People drank and sang and my friend danced with his cousins and his sisters and when things were their drunkenest and joyfulest, those kids came rushing back. Kicked in the backdoor like they were cops at a raid, and they just pounced on him. Five or six kids with butterfly knives just going nuts on him. He didn't stand a chance."

By now they've drifted out of the city into the foothills north of town. Beautiful dark country with a faint corona of red at the edges. Empty and sweet.

"That must have been a terrible thing to see."

Carl shrugs. "To be honest, I didn't even really know the guy. Just drove him from the prison to his sister's house. He was so happy to be free, he invited me along for the party."

They ride on silently for another few miles. It's well past two a.m. now and as they wind up and over the rising hills, that red glowing edge swells and brightens, ringed with the flashing lights of fire engines, all those culminating screaming sirens, and finally they're high enough to see a vast expanse of the foothills on fire. Crippled pitiful sagebrush and thistle. Barely surviving in the dust and sun. Now not surviving at all.

Parked along the shoulder of some barren scratch of road, they watch the faint shapes of engines and firemen fighting the overwhelming swath of flame, attacking something so massive and unstoppable. It will swallow the city whole. But in the few minutes they're there watching, Ben can see: they're pushing it back. The blind fury of fire somehow reigned in by little men with hoses and cherry-picker trucks.

"This whole affair," Carl says, gesturing to the spectacle, "is making me damn hungry, hoss."

"What, like a weenie roast?"

"Like roast chicken. Are you smelling this?"

By the time they ride back out of the foothills into the city, the fire's under control and something between them—within this cab, floating in the air—has changed. It feels better now than it did before. Earl and the grey men are forgotten. Everyone feels okay.

"Where should I drop you off?"

"Oh, just go wherever you're going, hoss. I can make my way home from there."

At the 777, the two shake hands in the parking lot and say goodbye, clap one another's shoulders, and as he climbs the stairs, grinning, still high, Ben glances down and for a moment sees it—is certain he's found it—an empty pool surrounded by parked cars, half-naked bodies spread out under the moon. For a moment he's proud to have found what he'd been promised and denied. Even when it disappears, he is proud.

On the upstairs walkway, outside his door and fumbling with his keys, Ben hears his name shouted from below. Leaning against the railing, he sees Carl still in the stark black and white of the parking lot lights, round face floating like a stained alabaster carving, standing right where the phantom pool had come and gone, stance wide like a fighter inviting the trouble of his enemy.

"Hey Ben," he calls again, and waits for Ben to answer. "You know who my friend was, right? The one who ran from his curse?"

"No," and he's smirking, is expecting a joke. "Who was your friend who ran from his curse?"

And Carl smiles. Broad and square-toothed. As if this really were a punch line. "Why, it was you." And he laughs. "You were the one." And he turns away, stride slow and casual, whistling something jaunty as he disappears into the night.

Chapter 8

"Sir? Señor?"

Cars lazily roll down the street, chased doggedly by a cool mountain breeze: rubber snarling thinly on gravel, the rattle of a cartwheeling shopping bag. Ben looks up at the waiter in white standing over him. Blinks a slow dry-eyed blink. Spreads his mouth in a dopey grin.

"Yes, sorry, um."

He had not meant to fall asleep.

"Is there anything else I can get for you, *pendejo*?"

There was a time when that wasn't quite the case.

The kid is dark and Latino and maybe all of sixteen years old. As far as Ben can remember, he has never seen this boy before in his life. Looking down at his table—at his plate with the sparse remains of pork and tortilla scraps, the scraped-clean dish of flan, three empty bottles of Negra Modelo, none of which he remembers ordering, let alone consuming—Ben purses his lips like a general inspecting the ravaged fields and slowly shakes his head.

"No, sir, I think I've done all the damage I can muster."

The kid clears the table, scoots inside to write up a bill, and Ben leans back in his chair, lets the afternoon's lazy near-silence pass over him like a dancer's undulating shawl, enjoys the sun and enjoys the breeze. There's no one else out here on the patio, most likely no one inside the restaurant either. Just Ben and the boy and whatever they decide exists between them. A little ways up the street, a shaggy eucalyptus rises up out of the cracked sidewalk. Parked in its shade, an old baby blue Cadillac quietly sleeps. The wind moves through the tree with a dry whispering rattle, and every now and then a leaf breaks free, flits through the air flashing silver and blue, silver and blue to land in tiny scallops on the Cadillac's hood and roof, and watching this quiet meditative dance, Ben nearly falls asleep again.

Which would be a shame. If he fell asleep again, Ben suspects, he'd forget all about this, too. Just like the lunch that appears to have been so enjoyed. Just like the journey that's led him to this place.

The bill comes and Ben leaves a generous tip pinned beneath a bottle of pepper sauce on the table, thanks the boy and strolls from the patio onto the sidewalk. Checks the time on his phone and wonders where the day has gone. Looks left and right and hears faintly the sound of traffic—engines and voices—to his right, so goes left.

He walks past the baby blue Cadillac stippled with leaves and light. He walks beneath the tree's hushing shade.

This neighborhood is new to him, sleepy and somehow both residential and slightly industrial. Bulldozers parked in the street. The acrid bite of hot asphalt in the air. Or maybe they're just repaving. A little farther along and the smell is gone and Ben adds these details to the map of his brain as around a bend and a little further on, he comes across a low complex of shops. Small parking lot

TO SLEEP AS ANIMALS

with faded painted lines. A mostly vacant marquee with a singular, quixotic listing, like some futurist cult,

THE REVERSE AGING CLUB

Ben crosses the parking lot, climbs the steps to the door and inside.

In the grey reflection in the door's window glass, Ben catches a momentary glimpse of himself, of his suit freshly dry-cleaned but baggy on him—he's losing weight—of his damaged mouth and how it's taking on the characteristics of road kill, ragged and crusted black at the edges. Overall, he looks washed up and battered but content, unembittered. Like any number of grey men before they resign themselves to the grey.

All the other shops inside, of course, are locked and unlit, cleared out or maybe never moved into. Ben tries the one open door and finds himself in a large room with two big cedar boxes up against the far wall, torturous machines in one corner and a floral dimness in the air. Like some hub or nexus, an unblinking woman stands at the center of the room.

"Hello," she says, and welcomes him to the club. Blonde and unwrinkled and completely unflinching in her gaze. As if she could see through him and was not surprised at what she saw. In the total countenance of her body and face, a vast potential for agelessness is spelled. Ben's glad to be wearing his one freshly laundered and unruined suit. "Do you have an appointment?"

"Um, no," and for no reason he digs his hands into his pockets. As if some evidence might come to hand. As if something on his person might justify his being here. "I just saw the sign out front and thought I'd come in."

"Well, we *are* a members-only club."

And before he can stop himself: "Do you really believe you can turn back time?"

The woman's expression does not change, in fact seems frozen but not unkindly. Minutely, she cocks her head to the right. Like she's trying to decipher a sign written in another language. Like maybe she did not see quite so clearly through him after all.

"We're a new-age health club," she finally explains. "The owner doesn't like me describing it that way—she'd probably prefer I use catchwords like 'healing' or 'shamanistic' or something—but that is in essence what we are about. Alternative medicine and spiritual health." And in a way that suggests she shouldn't offer—in fact wouldn't if the club were not deserted—she asks, "Would you like a tour?" and though her demeanor is still professional, it's obvious to Ben that the rules have changed and that she is the one who changed them.

"Um."

"Maybe you'll want to be a member once we're done." But even she seems to know better.

For a moment, Ben remembers sliding off the branch above the stream, remembers giving in to gravity's guiding downward pull. The release of relinquishing control.

"Fuck it." And he smiles. "Let's see what you've got to offer."

If time can move backwards, maybe gravity can, too. Maybe there is up-ness after all. In quick animal motions, the woman hurries to a boom box on a shelf near the cedar boxes, snaps off the ethereal synthesized music Ben hadn't noticed was playing until it wasn't. She scans the room as if looking for a place to begin, then pours him a paper cone of water from a cooler in the corner.

"Thank you."

"It's alkaline water."

"I see." He wonders if he wasn't meant to drink it, was meant instead to rinse his hands, anoint his brow.

"It's *very* good for you."

"Of course."

As she leads him and his water through the club, it becomes clear to Ben that this space was once an office, set up with phone jacks and power outlets everywhere, drop ceilings and sockets where sterile florescent lights once ran. Someday someone will again wheel in dividers, build cubicles, answer phones. Meanwhile, the woman shows him a tray containing what appears to be a poorly rolled and mostly burnt-up joint of hash. "This is all the junk," she explains, "your ears can release after just one candling."

"You burn candles in your ears."

"In a sense, yes."

"Wouldn't that make more wax?"

She stares at him and blinks once, intentionally, but as she sets down the tray he sees her secretly smile.

He allows her to candle his ears. "As a demonstration." She lights a cone of waxed paper first in one ear, then the other, catching the ash and wax drippings in a separate tray while he sits awkwardly upright beside her in a small chamber that, in another life, was probably a broom closet.

"All this junk," she says when they're done, pointing at the yellow deposits, "was inside your head." The alluvium is the same beehive yellow of the waxed paper cone. "It clogs your senses." Ben pokes at the debris but says nothing. "Makes thinking impossible."

She offers to let him keep what came out of him. He kindly declines her offer.

The torture equipment turns out to be unwieldy exercise machines that, when demonstrated, flail the woman's limbs around like a rag doll inside a thresher. The cedar boxes are infrared saunas that, she claims, are better for you than steam saunas. But when he asks her how they're better or why, she just smiles. A mouthful of teeth so clearly designed for biting.

She shows him her private office, a sterile white cell where she practices massage and waxing and cosmetic tattooing as additional services for club members.

"Cosmetic tattooing?"

"Permanent makeup. Lip color. Eye shadow. Blush," and she points to her upper lip. "I gave myself this beauty mark."

He squints at the tiny mole near the corner of her mouth. "Nice." And because she seems to expect something more: "Very strategically placed."

And for one fleeting second, she breaks out of character and laughs. "I'm sorry, but you are terrible at this."

"I know!"

"It's like you've never talked to a person before."

"It's true, I'm inadequate at this human business."

In this tight space of bright lights and paper-draped table, isopropyl and cotton swabs, their laughter reverberates and pings into the corners. Momentarily, they regain their composed and serious faces.

"As a demonstration," she asks, "would you like me to wax your unibrow?"

"Not on your life."

"Let me show you the chi machine," and straight-faced, she leads him back into the main room.

Ben expects an expansive contraption, something hidden until a secret switch is flipped, walls grinding open, sliding apart, revealing some capsule that will swallow him whole, beam radiation through him and purify his aura. Instead, she leads him to a private nook where a mat is rolled out on the floor. She instructs him to lie down and rest his ankles in the padded cradle of a small black box at his feet.

"This is the chi machine," she says of the box, gently stretching Ben's arms out above his head. "This will realign your chakras." And she switches on the machine.

Humming softly, the machine fluidly glides his ankles from side to side, side to side, the waving motion traveling up his legs, into his body and out his arms. He feels like a wriggling worm. Kneeling beside him, the woman sets colored stones over his heart, on his belly and near his groin, reciting the properties of each piece as she places it on his body. "This is topaz," she stage whispers. "This will harness your sun energy." This, he wants to tell her, is so clearly bullshit and you know it. But he keeps up the game, makes quiet sounds that he hopes convey enlightenment and minor epiphany. As the machine wags his body, some of the stones slip off.

Then, without warning, the machine clicks off. Yet still, through his body, he feels it continue to shake him. "You feel that?" The echo of the machine sounding through him. "That's your chakra singing." And until the sensation wears off, he almost believes her. "That's your soul falling back in place."

Ben does not purchase a membership with the Reverse Aging Club. Instead, he thanks her for the tour, shakes her hand, and the woman plays along to the very end when she asks if he'd like her business card and instead hands him a coupon for a free wheat grass juice, redeemable at any area Smoothie Queen.

"If you have any questions," she says, beaming, "about anything, don't be afraid to call."

Ben pockets the coupon with a conspiratorial wink. "You'll be hearing from me soon."

"I better!"

Her laughter trails after him as he steps out into the afternoon sun and breeze.

NORTH AND EAST OF the city, the landscape thins like the edges of an unfinished painting until there are no trees and there are no houses, just an open expanse of unpeopled prairie eventually leading up to a metal and glass facility surrounded by a grassy patchwork of plots and grazing cows. Ben pulls through the facility gates and parks where he can, steps out into the declining light and straightens the lines of his slacks and jacket, the lay of his tie, walks across the lot and through the front door. Inside, he asks the receptionist if he could please see Dr. Elizabeth Fanning, please, and with a shellacked grin the receptionist zips out from behind her desk and guides him down a hall, past several laboratories and out a backdoor into a paddock where El stands petting the orange and white shanks of dew-eyed Guernsey cow.

She smiles when she sees him crossing carefully through the lush pasture grass. Eyes laughing even when her voice is not. All things interpreted as play. In a long white lab coat and a single rubber glove stretched bluely to her elbow.

"Hello, cousin," she says, hugging him awkwardly so as not to touch him with her gloved hand. But now, so close, the laughter drops from her eyes like pennies into a well. "Jesus, Ben, what'd you do to your mouth?"

He touches the tear in his lip, feels the faint glistening wet of pus or blood. "Fell down the motel stairs the other night. Smacked my lip on the railing."

"You need to get that cleaned up."

"It'll be fine, I'm sure."

Her body rises and falls with a momentous sigh: he can see her wanting to argue the point, can see her struggling to put it aside, and when she has to physically shake the concern from her head, a flashing hungover sickness passes through his belly. It doesn't seem fair that she has to care so much. Her eyes are bright with laughter again when she gestures to the hulking creature beside them.

"Ben, I'd like you to meet G-1314, or as I like to call her, Miss Alice."

The cow looks up to blink at Ben, and when she does, he swears, a fat tear races from her eye and off her furry jaw.

"Does she always look so forlorn?"

"She's allergic to something in blossom right now. Probably musk thistle. Aren't you, girl?"

The cow blinks out another doleful tear. When he scratches the wide gap between her eyes, she nuzzles his hand once, then returns to the earnest business of chewing her cud.

"Alice is the representative from her test herd," El explains. "She's the one my team runs all its tests on, to see how her herd is responding."

"Responding to what?" It occurs to Ben that he has almost no idea what El does here. What her profession entails. What her life's all about.

"Their diet, mainly. We have dozens of test herds grazing on specific wild grasses, and also some that subsist mainly on pelletized grains and other processed foods. At this one facility there are dozens of different research teams running tests to determine everything from milk production to meat quality."

On either side of them stand other, identical paddocks, some with cows grazing alone or occasionally in the company of a white coat. Most are empty.

"But that's not what you do here."

"No, I'm more interested in what's actively going on inside Alice. My team and I are trying to determine how well the herds respond to specific diets, which foods they can most readily digest, et cetera."

"And how do you do that?"

"Well, in Alice's case, by looking," and leading Ben around the cow, she shows him the porthole installed in Alice's opposite flank. Stainless steel and thick window glass. A beige paste slowly churning behind the pane.

"You guys cut a window into a cow."

"It's a surgical procedure like any other. We shave and sterilize the area and put her under with a common anesthesia, keep her comfortable and lazy and pleasantly medicated for a few days while she recovers. The same way they'd install a pacemaker or a hip replacement in you or me."

She reaches into her jacket's deep pocket, produces another rubber glove. "It allows us access to one of her stomachs, which in turn allows us to test the bolus and check out what's going on inside her."

"What could you possibly gain," he asks, "from looking inside a cow's stomach?"

El hands him the glove. "All kinds of things." Then she opens Alice's porthole.

He takes the glove but does not intend to use it. He puts on the glove and gazes into the open belly. He cannot do this. He decides: he cannot do this. The universe and its varied components have created all these lines and barriers, some easily crossed and some more difficult and some that, by their very nature, should not be crossed. A bullet into a brain. A hand inside a body.

Ben puts his hand into the cow's stomach.

"See? Is that so bad?"

Inside is warm and softly moving. Through the open porthole, a faint organic breath like a brewer's mash puffs out. Unaware of the hand in her belly, Alice chews her cud and gazes blankly into the middle distance. As if the cement mixer of her stomach does not want to let him go, when

Ben tries to take back his hand, he has to fight to pull it free.

"Now you've one more thing," El says, "to include in the compendium of your research." And she carefully hasps shut the porthole.

"But what's the point of doing this?" He's holding his gloved hand away from his body like it's something foreign and contaminated. "What good is a window into an animal's belly?"

"I can take samples," she says, helping him out of his soiled glove, "and from studying those samples find out how efficiently the cow is digesting its particular diet."

"But what's important about that?"

"The better they digest their food," and with a hand on his back, she leads him away from the cow, "the less methane they each produce."

"Methane?"

Hers and his making a single pair, she drops their soiled gloves into a biological waste bin by the door.

"Methane."

Holding the door open, she follows him into the building.

"There are several million cattle in this county alone, most of whom are raised for beef and all of whom create a tremendous amount of methane. Methane, of course, is a greenhouse gas. Now, if we could convince everyone in America to go vegetarian or, at the very least, consume less beef, the problem would not be quite so severe. Given the likelihood of that ever happening, my team and I are trying to find a rumen diet that results in the least methane possible."

"You're trying to save the world," he says.

"I'm trying," she says, "to do something useful while playing with microscopes and animals. I'm justifying my need to have fun. Which means that, before we go, I need to tie up a couple loose ends here. I shouldn't be too long. Think you can stay out of trouble for a few minutes?"

He smiles, says nothing either way, and El slips back out into Alice's paddock.

Waiting, meandering through the facility's halls, Ben peeks into the labs he passes, hoping to find something interesting and horrendous but mostly finding darkened rooms, the occasional body hunched over a paper-strewn desk, once someone pouring with curious imprecision various liquids into a series of glass beakers. He listens for any sense to be made out of what conversations he might overhear, behind doors or around corners. "The lactate sample from H-4110 was positively chartreuse. Only a Mennonite would find that appealing." So far, he finds there's no sense to be made.

He's at the end of a corridor on the second floor, reading the postings on a page-littered bulletin board—rooms for rent and student bands performing in abandoned barns, opportunities for internships and anthropomorphized animal cartoons—when his phone zaps a single sudden joy-buzzer in his pocket. Trotting downstairs, Ben finds El waiting in the entryway foyer in a peachy cotton blouse and green skirt, hair up but no makeup, not really needing it, not looking at all like she's just had her hands inside a living animal's body, and looking at her Ben feels a warm clenching below his belly that both ignites and repels him. He tries to ignore it, returns his cousin's laughing smile. He offers his elbow and they walk, arms linked, out the doors into the crepuscular air.

As they climb into his slouching Jeep, Ben hopes he's been successful in blowing the lingering scent of grey men out the windows into the desert vacuum. But when they get in and start driving, all he can smell is El's faint perfume.

"Orange blossoms?"

"You prefer Guernsey?"

The sky is a patchwork of flimsy white clouds that hold no hope of rain. On the road they ride without speaking for a while before El finally asks to change the radio station. The dial is still lost somewhere between new wave and soul, notes and voices vulcanized by static. Ben had begun to enjoy the shipwreck of sound.

She finds a station playing jug-town blues. Descending from the pastures into the darkening city, they listen to thin tin-can voices singing about sisters killing sisters to win the affections of paramourous suitors, of madmen making fiddles from the bones of dead girls, oh the terrible wind and rain.

Ben imagines anyone committing murder for the sake of his affection. He imagines being murdered to clear the way for another's love.

In some anonymous suburban mallscape south and east of downtown, they pull into the parking lot of a huge grey box with Asian writing on the street-side sign. An emerald and gold mural of a dragon surrounded by Noh theater figures on the sun-bleached outside wall. A neon sign of a squid and a shark. Inside has the feel of one unending and amazing caliginous expanse interrupted periodically by soft islands of clean light: a half moon bar with a chef inside the crescent, white-robed and swiftly chopping. The scent of ginger and, faintly, brewed soy. El speaks with the hostess, who disappears into the miasmic dark, leaving them waiting by her station. Ben feels as though they're drifting on a raft through a midnight archipelago, through some ocean in a dream. They cast no shadows within this sea of black. Beside him, El smiles and squeezes his hand, teeth faintly illuminated like bones in the dark. "You'll enjoy this, I swear." The hostess returns and, speaking so softly as to almost make no sound, leads them to their island.

And still, that drifting sensation. As if the floor had a lapping purl, a trough and a crest. Marooned and led by a whispering ghost. Even in the light, they cast no shadows. The chef in their island is brown-skinned and compact with smiling almond eyes, and though his voice is clear and crisp as a rain-wet bell, Ben again cannot understand one word the man grins in greeting.

"We're wonderful, thank you," El tells him. "We'll each have a Sapporo, I guess, and a carafe of hot sake to split while we wait for our friends, please."

As the chef prepares their drinks, Ben looks over the scroll-worked shelf dividing the bar's inner contour from the outer. Bamboo mats and myriad knives. Bowls of orange pearls and long lengths of vibrant fish meat: red and gold and white and pink. Ben eyes El, who beams excited as a child at him. Under the counter, she pinches the skin above his knee.

"I forget what a northeastern white boy you are sometimes."

"I'm so lost here, kiddo."

"I'll take care of you, don't worry."

"I'm counting on it."

The chef presents them their drinks and a plate with two oysters on the half-shell, raw and dotted with flakes of scallion greens. Drops of lemon juice shine like singing voices. "While you wait for your friends," he says, and turns away, busies himself cleaning something that may or may not be dirty.

El pours the sake and as a silent toast, they touch shells and swallow their oysters, drink a shot, fall into a meditative silence, lips salted and bellies warming, and when two new figures emerge from the darkness El stands and hugs them each in turn—first the woman, then the man—introduces them to Ben, and though he tries not to, he forgets their names even as he shakes their hands.

The new couple sits and orders some drinks, and after a brief discussion as to what they should drink to, they raise a toast to Voyager's safe passage as it imminently slips outside our sun's house. While El and the man settle to the task of deciding what to order, the woman—black-eyed and black hair and skin deeply tanned or maybe simply dark—tells Ben about a lecture she just heard at the university, a brief talk given by two Native American sisters, Western Shoshone grandmothers whose land was confiscated under allegations of overgrazing.

"The government is stealing their horses," she says, "and commandeering huge tracts of wild grazing land, then turning it immediately over to a gold mining operation." She pauses to let this bombshell explode, her mouth a limp O of shock, but her eyes shine like some undersea mammal's, infinite and deep. "I mean, what century are we even in?"

"What would the government do," he asks, "with a herd of stolen horses?"

Under the bar, again, El pinches him, and before the woman can reply, the chef reappears in their island's tropical moonlight to take their order, mentally cataloging El's list of foreign sounds.

"What's an *unagi*?"

"I can't believe you've never done this before."

He pours four more shots of sake.

"I like to stick to things I understand."

But she doesn't even grace him with the favor of playing along. It's almost mean, the way she laughs.

The food comes in small waves, on footed rectangular plates, vivid constructions of rice and fish, seaweed and roe. They strike a balanced ratio of eating, drinking, and blathering so that no one seems to ever get full or drunk or bored with each story that rises up but never concludes, only diffusing into something else. Lines connecting stars. Shapes among clouds. The man tells a story about someone he met while hiking in Yosemite—tall and skeletal and far too emaciated to be attempting any climb, let alone Half-Dome—and in the narrative web it becomes clear to Ben a danger is imminent, something unavoidable and catastrophic looming over the horizon, yet he cannot follow the man's verbal path. The sound of his voice blends with the light shining on his face, in the dark eyes of his companion, on the skin of El's arm and neck. In his head, the sake has built a warm gauzy nest, as if he were somewhere between a waking memory and a dream, and this too melds with the light and music of these voices, this place. He becomes a receptacle for indiscriminant sensation. He wonders if this is how synesthesia feels.

The chef presents them with what appears to be a giant green caterpillar posing majestic, body segmented in avocado slices, eyes of orange unblinking roe, and even as it is deconstructed by nipping chopsticks, there's something mesmerizing in its shape and color, how it reflects the light, and even as he sincerely though inadvertently speaks aloud—"I want to keep this, I want a picture"—and their laughter breaks out around him, breaks out with him because sincerity is such a silly thing, he becomes aware of El beside him, leaning into him, her shoulder and back pressed to his chest, almost in his lap, almost with his arm around her, and it occurs to him that this—the two of them with this couple, eating and drinking in some otherworldly light and space—is a playful act of public theater. Taking on roles outside their full, natural roles. While shaking hands and giving hugs, no one said anything about blood relations. In this place, he is no one's cousin.

"So what do you do, Ben?" the man asks, jerking him back to the moment.

"Ben's a visiting researcher," El explains, "embedded in the university."

"Embedded, huh?" The man wipes his mouth with a napkin and smiles. "Sounds painful. What are you researching?"

Ben looks down at the top of the table without moving his head, creates without intending to the image of a somniloquist, as if speaking under hypnosis. "How certain phenomena can be reshaped," he says, "by changes in light and sound. How changing how you hear and see something can effect a desired outcome." When he looks at them, his eyes become coins half lost in the fountain. "How vast the ambiguities are in how any value can be judged."

"Sounds fascinating."

"What," the woman asks, "does that even mean?"

"It means," El says, "we could all be part of his research." And they laugh and eat and Ben pleasantly falls again into the role of prop in a scene, catching the light, creating a balance in form and content, seeing and being seen, and even after the double date is over and Ben is driving El back to her home, is in her yard and inside her house, the feeling persists. The feeling persists but is soon gone, and as they lie naked on their sides in her bed, her back to his belly and his face nestled in her neck, in her hair, pressed to her shoulders and spine, he feels himself become something else, engaged and engaging, the opposite of a prop.

Their bottom arms stretch out and up to where their hands clasp. His free hand caresses her foothill of hip, the plain of her belly, reading her text of skin in fingertip and tongue while her free hand moves between her parted thighs, stroking where his own sex moves against hers, pressing his against hers, finally grasps and guides him inside, and even as they move together, inside and surrounding one another, she continues to stroke his sex and her sex and the point where the two unite and Ben feels like anything but a prop. They move with one another like constituent parts to an improvised ritual dance, and even when it's over and he feels himself slackening inside her, she holds her hand to their union, keeps him inside her body as long as she possibly can.

ON THE FIRST DAY of school with his father's new rules, Ben found he could not talk to anyone, could not find a safe way to interact at all. Even activities that did not directly break any rule—to not touch, to not speak out of turn—he could see eventually leading to any and all parameters of proper conduct being destroyed. So he spoke to no one. He stayed as far away from the other kids as he could.

And as he watched them run and tackle and play, he realized he was not one of them. His rules were different because he was different. Not a child or even a human but something meant to observe all the ways in which everyone else operated and behaved. All the things he could never be. Lying now with El—still back to belly, still inside her, still tangled in her body—he wonders why he never rebelled against this. Why he changed the language but never the spirit. Why he never chose to be like everyone else.

El's free hand strokes his shoulder now as he holds her closely, his arms knit across her breasts, and as they sow together in this human knot, he notices that his skin and her skin are so different in hue as to be different things altogether, not even comparable, yet still he asks her, "How can you be so much darker than me?" and she answers him honestly, directly, never treating him like a joke when he doesn't mean to be.

"It's because you were raised in the arctic," she says, "and I was raised somewhere habitable."

"I thought deserts were supposed to be life-taking places."

To Sleep as Animals

"Mm. Mm-hmm. Yet life got its toehold in Mesopotamia."

It's one of those nights where it's hotter in the dark than in the day. He can feel their sweat mingling where they touch. Where you were raised, he thinks incompletely, where I was raised…. Where his crotch is pressed against her, he can feel their commingled fluids wet and cooling as evidence and before he can say anything—before the words can burble up and out like a drowning man's last released breath—she shushes him, pulls him against her and shushes him, "Don't, Ben, it's okay, you don't—" and he makes some sound like a dying animal and she shushes him again. "It's nothing." She rolls over and holds him to her chest, clasping, stroking his hair. "If it was any other time it wouldn't mean a thing."

But how can anyone imagine events unfolding under some other clock or calendar's reign? We would each be someone else. So different as to be unrecognizable. His body is a quiver, his breath a falling leaf. We wouldn't even be who we are anymore.

As he falls asleep against her, he faintly hears her say, "It'd be expected," and he's gone.

A DOG RUNNING IN its sleep, feet kicking, faintly yelping. Waking itself at the sound of its own bark. At some point in the night, Ben wakes and lies silently in the dark of El's room. Beside him, her breath is a slow shallow tide, her body a shoreline. Careful not to wake her, Ben slips out of bed, gathers his clothes and dresses in the living room, quietly steps out into the night air where the heat has finally—mercifully—broken, a hand of cool air tranquilizing the valley.

Walking past the equestrian park and up Pioneer, onto Skyline and past the firehouse, Ben crosses the cool grass of the adjacent park, bypassing the playground and aiming for the edge overlooking the reservoir canal. The houses on the canyon's opposite bank. The distant casino lights. The city at large. But before he gets too far something moves beneath his foot—jets away in a flurry from under his stepping heel—and Ben backpedals, freezes, heart pounding, sure the ground has come alive to slither beneath him. It takes a moment for him to register, just barely silhouetted in the diffuse streetlight, the nearby shape of a rabbit or desert hare. Unmoving but for the rapid-fire pulse of its breath. Slowly, Ben takes one careful step toward it, then another, and again, it does not move until he's nearly stepped on it, and it flees.

Surrounded in the dark, Ben becomes aware of many rabbits or hare. Barely moving, barely there to move. Eyes faint red and reflecting. Why have they all gathered here? It becomes a trick walking to the edge with them barely escaping underfoot. The sickening anticipation of this one—this next one—not making it in time. Never being able to see them until they've already fled. Somehow, Ben makes it to the edge. Far below, the water is a whisper, a promise, a wish. The city a silent jewel all around. Ben carefully seeks the trail down.

Good and evil only make sense, he thinks as he descends the canyon trail, in the context of one another. Neither can exist without the other. Equal and opposite. Each dies in the absence of the other. So if a mask of pure evil destroys all innocence, then isn't its aim self-erasure? We destroy the good to dispel the evil. Don the mask and erase the blackboard. Reset everything to zero.

When he and El walked the canal that first afternoon—as they walked back to her house and up from the canyon's deepest belly and slope—he noticed that, at some points, the water ran uphill.

"It's a new design in civil engineering," she answered when he asked. "Anti-gravity rays. I don't know how they do it."

Descending now along the trail, skittering on loose stones, Ben decides he will answer his own question. He will find this water's poisoned source. He will determine what makes it flow. But down here, away from the street lamps and scattered lights, Ben can barely see, stumbles and slips, at some point realizes he's lost the trail, and as something catches his foot and he falls for real, pitching forward and down with sickening finality into the cool creek water, it occurs to him all at once that maybe this was, after all, not a very good idea.

But I'm here, he tells himself, even as the dull ache of his twisted ankle makes itself known. I've made it this far. He wades into the canal and tries to lie on the surface, to float facedown, to let the

To Sleep as Animals

current carry him along. If I can't find its source, then I will find its goal. But all he does is sink. He's no longer a boy dazzled by sun and gravity, no longer a particle in a much greater stream. He has weight now. He bears orbits of his own, and anyway, this water is too shallow for anything like floating.

Ben feels the burden of his selfhood. In this valley, soaked and broken and reminded again of what he is and is not. A researcher failing at his research. Unwilling to believe in what his evidence proves. Denying what he finds in the light in lieu of the safe ambiguity of the dark. At best an alcoholic and at worst a somnambulistic narcoleptic, an amnesiac who doesn't know what he doesn't know. The sort of man who consorts with dim strangers while avoiding the people he loves. Hurting his friends. Fucking his cousin. Failing and failing and failing. Washed in the canal's slow purl, he feels these facts stack up in a pale monument to everything he'd rather not know. He longs to be rid of this weight.

Clothes river-wet and cold, left foot a new tender thing to watch out for: it's a long walk out of the canyon.

Chapter 9

Limping back up the reservoir trail, Ben imagines how easy it would be to go back to El's house. Allow himself in. Leave his sopping clothes on her porch and wash himself in her shower. Dry off with her towel. Tiptoe into her room and crawl into her bed beside her. Soak in her scent permeating the sheets. Nestle his body alongside her body and breathe in her sleep and her warmth. He imagines waking up beside her as dawn paints diamonds through the curtained window and onto her bed, her face, her bright morning eyes open and watching him. It would be so easy to stay. To lie in bed with her as morning took on the full vestments of day. To cook breakfast with her in her kitchen and eat beside her on her porch while across the street, horses cantered through the grass, their snorts and breath hanging as a haze in the air. All these things, this imagined life with El that, whether he likes it or not, he's already dipped his toe into, this thing that terrifies him by being what it is, yet somehow still feels so... *normal.* All of it, he knows, is a choice. He could block the calls from Syracuse, burn all his notebooks, hawk his camera and his clever carbon-fiber gun. That's a choice he could make. She could be his center. From her anchor, he could float free. That could be his choice. It'd be so easy to stay.

When Ben steps up and out of the canyon, ankle swelling and split lip reopened, black syrup of blood trickling down his chin, he wrestles with his wet pocket until he finds his keys, puts the Jeep in neutral and pushes it out of her driveway, pushes it another half-block down the street before starting the engine and driving away.

AT THE 777, HE RAIDS the Quikie Mart for whatever seems of any true utility. Mostly cheap bottles of whiskey, sliced cheese and a spongy loaf of factory-pressed white bread. Packets of black pens and a map of Nevada. As an impulse, he also buys an ancient-looking bottle of white glue. He hoards his provisions under the bed in his room. He hangs a DO NOT DISTURB sign on the outside knob. He keeps the deadbolt locked.

For three days, he does not leave his room. Or anyway, does not remember leaving. There are big blank gaps in his memory: it's too convenient, he knows, to call them blackouts. But at some point a computer printout appears on top of his stack of compiled research and notes, copied from some historical index and listing countless towns throughout the Nevada desert that had been incorporated then abandoned. And within the long blank vacancies, there are flashes of memory. The dull glass and steel cube of the library south of town, dark angles impressed against the sky. The winking lights around the Silver Legacy's marquee burning white then dark and burning again. Plastic bags swishing like tumbleweeds down windswept streets. People laughing. People stepping away. And anyway, again or later, a bag of frozen peas appears duct-taped to his wounded ankle. He lies in bed and drinks a glass of whiskey from a stale-tasting coffee mug while the swelling in his upraised foot, he hopes, goes down. When the peas thaw, he eats them like candy from the bag.

And it's obvious to him during this time that he has become a tremendous mess. For a day his various notebooks and napkin scrawls scatter across his bed in stacks and regions, as if lines demarcated one set of research from another. But in a drunken late-night fit, he tears the piles apart, ripping pages from their spiral bindings and tossing them around the room, kicking the litter like snow, destroying the evidence of his labors and failures, though later, pooling the pages together, he begins to reassemble his findings. Just not in their previous order. He rereads his mostly incomprehensible scrabble, underlines phrases, circles details, rewrites entire sections, collects thematically-related passages together in bundles and stacks, takes notes on his notes, creates a cataloging system in the margins of the nightstand's Gideon Bible.

He finds many entries he does not remember writing. A list describing people's hands:

- *long narrow fingers that move as though missing a joint*
- *the short square digits of a carpenter or dwarf*
- *arthritic claws, a squatting bird*
- *a child's paw squirming from a grown man's wagging wrist*

A list of voices. A list of eyes. No names are attached to any entry.

In one snowdrift of ripped-apart pages, Ben finds the notes he took on Ethyl upon first meeting her:

> *former dancer—voice like ruined corduroy—black shape in the lounge—contempt for weak, shortsighted—cannot id. w/self-inflicted suffering—nigerian man in a great death mask—no <u>body</u> inside—indiv. erased by persona assumed—ghost town, LUNDY, Mono Lake—business men & whores chasing railroads across the*

> *country—avalanches & fires—the*
> *line where loss outweighs any gain*

Later he finds an almost identical account of their meeting (*avalanche—whores & housefires—your shadow disappears until the mask sets you free*), but where the first note names the ghost town Lundy, the second calls it Bodie. One account's written on a tattered scrap of bar napkin. One's written on a torn college-rule page. And now, vaguely, he remembers her talking about a ghost town south of here, near the salt pylons on Mono Lake, remembers asking her about ghost towns and she only knew of the one. "Outside the tourist traps and movie sets, anyway. If that's what you want, the Ponderosa Ranch is just in Carson City or so." He remembers her saying these words. But what town was she talking about?

He finds neither Bodie nor Lundy on his map of Nevada. He finds both listed and circled on his ghost town listing.

The swelling in his ankle gets worse. Pressure, he decides, is what he needs. Pressure is key. He rips apart one of his T-shirts until it's one long ragged length, then binds his purpling foot. He cinches the wrap as tight as he can, tugging the knot closed with his teeth.

Meanwhile, the bathtub fills with empty pint bottles. Walker's Deluxe and Ancient Age. Everything—the pages, the darkness and the light—everything is touch and go.

At some point Ben finds himself, as if just waking, holding onto the railing along the 777's second floor tier, looking out over the parking lot below, the night sky a vast and empty threat as the city lights stare out bright and vacant all around. Behind him, the door hangs open, exhales onto the breeze the flat stink of old socks and spilt booze. He's naked from the waist up, barefoot, clammy with sweat. In his right hand is a white cardstock square.

> OUR CONCERN IS THAT YOU ARE DESPERATE TO DISPROVE WHAT WE HAVE SENT YOU WEST TO PROVE.

Slowly, he turns the square over to read what's printed on its other side.

> WE DID NOT MAIL YOU TO YOUR COUSIN'S DOORSTEP FOR NOTHING, MISTER NIGRA.

Ben folds the letter in an uneven half and slides it into his pocket. Below, not even on the streets does he see a single moving soul. But for these men writing oblique letters to him, far away: all alone. Yet still, he creeps back into his room, steps quietly, as if afraid someone might wake at the lock's metallic snick.

There are countless notes on the Tahoe snow plant. Most report the same ideas over and over again. As if contemplating the nature of a plant incidental to his research might somehow illuminate…what? *If the relationship is parasitic*, several entries conjecture,

> *between the Indian pipe and its constituent bacteria, the former has to be the parasite. Removed from the labors of its bacterial host, it would unilaterally wither and die. Yet of the two parties, the Indian pipe is the one who, by nature, is immobile. Fixed firmly in its landscape. The bacteria are free to move throughout the soil. Yet they chose to stay. Remain fastened to the Indian pipe's roots. Thus: a symbiosis. But what does the bacteria gain?*

And elsewhere, later:

> *Who determines what a benefit might be? Who decides the nature of a relationship?*

On the third day, Ben emerges from the stale yawn of his room, not even certain if it'll be day or night he steps into, is surprised to find the sun just setting, the air purple and transparent and ghostly. As if the day itself were haunting the spare gorges and cliffs of the earth.

Downstairs, he stops at the Quikie Mart for a candy bar and a bottle of water, and when he steps back out onto the street he sees a handful of grey men gathered, cow-like and social among one another but quieting when they see him, shying away. As if he carries something under his skin that even they want to avoid.

"What's up, fellas?" He pulls long and thirstily from his bottle as he approaches. They mumble hellos. They do not try to look near him. "What's new?" Then: "Haven't seen anyone for a few days." And finally, when none says a word, "Have any of you seen Earl recently?" And though still not one of them speaks, they look at him, all red-eyed and staring, and in their stares he reads their accusation. Even these men, he thinks, have discovered what I am. Even they know me now. He leaves the grey men on the corner and gets in his Jeep, heads for the highway, drives east.

Beside him in the passenger seat, he has a list. Ophir 1 and Ophir 2. Bodie or Lundy. Silver mines and reduction mills and places he's already forgotten. He sets out on the highway to X out the names on his list.

In the silence of I-80, he adjusts the dial until the duets no one ever meant to compose or hear come bleeding through the crackling speakers. She's on her knees and he's following you, Big River. You'll dump his blues down in the Gulf and she will take him there.

For the first few miles, things are clear. The fresh water feels good in his mouth and veins, icy and pure, an inoculation or even a cure. The sign posts thin out as he draws farther from the city. Beyond the wavering arc of his headlights: darkness. When the shakes come on like a butterfly quiver seated deep in the marrow of his bones, it's all he can do to pull off to the shoulder, leave the engine idling, the music, the static. He closes his eyes, head convulsing against the back of the seat as the buffeting wind slams the Jeep—a passing semi, a dragon, a train—tries to keep his breath steady, breath calm, and sliding in a crouch to the floor beneath the dash, eventually, mercifully, he sleeps.

But of course, when he wakes, he's not where he thought he would be.

IN THE PURPLE TWILIGHT east of Silver Springs, Ben makes it out of the barroom into the bland deep-fryer-and-beer stink of the parking lot before vomiting under the halo of door-light, hugging one-handed his bulging paper bag and clutching his marked-up map, leaning against the entryway frame. Moths bounce around his head beneath the mercury-vapor lamp. He pukes again, discharging from someplace deeper than his belly a thick yellow stream, viscous and hot like stomach acid and snot. It burns in the rough gash in his lip. It makes him want to cry. The moths circle and spin. He makes sure not to drop the bag. When it's over and he can catch his breath, he sees the sticky splatter on the pavement and half expects it to slither away and escape. He leaves it before it can leave him.

In his Jeep, under the lot's one flickering arc-sodium lamp, Ben takes inventory. He takes a long calming drink from one of the three bottles the bartender sold him. Then he studies the network of penned-ink Xs on his map.

Sometimes it feels like he's in two places at once. Hauling through the dark toward the bruised squint of dawn, yet also in his room at the 777. Peering through the dark of some gutted bunker dug underneath the crusted scale of the desert floor. Kicking empty cans from around graffitied ruins. Squinting in the August sun.

Sometimes, he feels as if he's in multiple times. Trapped in the ticking heart of a hidden clock. He could be anywhere.

On the radio, Bono sees the stones set in your eyes. Counterpoint on the radio, George Harrison sees the love here that's sleeping. But when Ben turns down a narrow pass between mountains, it's the static that sings the truest note.

When he wakes again, it's dawn and he's bunched up on the floor beneath the Wagoneer's dashboard. Outside, the sunlight is an autoclave.

Sterilizing the earth. He's certain, if he goes out there, it will kill him.

But when he sits up and squints out the window, he finds he's at the Ophir Mill ghost town that he and El once explored. Not just parked near it or within walking distance but in the settlement itself. Next to the tiny cemetery. Right in front of a fallen-in home.

Autoclave or not: Ben steps out into the sun.

FURTHER EAST THAN he's ever been within the sprawling Nevada desert, Ben finds the remains of an alleged ghost town. A pile of stones that might have been a foundation or might have been a fire pit. A collapsed well. The open old-man mouth of an abandoned mine. He tries to find any trace that someone—anyone—fought to save the life they'd built in this place. But no evidence suggests any kind of holding on. Only leaving.

He walks into the mine deep enough for the light to leave him. He stands in the cool silk and lung of the dark. A faint stale wind blows from deep inside the mine, icy and mineral, the breath of the ancient world. He tries to leave himself open to whatever ghosts might still be trapped here. But mostly, he feels safe in his blindness.

HE DOESN'T BOTHER with the collapsing buildings with their windows punched out and blind. Doesn't bother with the wind-scoured cemetery remains. There's only one reason to ever come back here. Squinting against the poison of the sun, Ben follows the talus grade up the canyon face, to the twin gaps carved through the stone.

YET SOMEHOW, TOO, he's back in his room working on his Gideon Index, updating and revising entries—crossing out the line between El's facility and the flea-tortured dog, cross-referencing them both with the highway-side bunker—in a leaky black ink. Biting the pen's wet nib, thinking of how best to reassemble a phrase, he sees on the windowsill's edge, stuffed roughly inside a Dixie cup, the feeble growth of a tiny

Indian pipe. Greying red and petals limp. He's proud that it hasn't died yet.

ONE GHOST TOWN IS little more than a broken-hinged outhouse tucked up in the rocky hills. Below, bolted to a stone, a brass plaque so worn by sand and wind it can't even be read, the words a thin suggestion nubbling an otherwise smooth metal face. Before noon, he finds another abandoned settlement that actually seems to have once existed in the lives and memories of human beings. Several burnt-out houses and a water tower. A library with moldering books on cracked and sagging shelves. On a sheet of plywood nailed over a storefront window, someone has written in long-faded brushstrokes of black paint, *SAVE US*. It's the most hopeful shred of evidence he's found so far.

THE CELLOPHANE COVERING the pictures in the pages of his album does not so much peel off as crumble between his fingers. The old paste cracks and falls away in a dust. As evidence, he glues his pictures into his Gideon Index. Black and white or sepia-tone. The faces of family long dead. Ben peels away and reattaches his pictures, from the album in his luggage to the Bible in his lap, and with each picture he recognizes some element of himself. His mom at five in shades of red. His mom at eight, in a dress and sitting on the lawn. His grayscale dad by an azalea bush in full bloom, his sweater too short to fully cover the round bulge of his belly, and another in the same spot with his little sister—Ben's aunt, El's mother—and they can't be more than four and five years old.

His grandmother as a virgin. His grandmother as a bride. His dad's parents holding hands on a porch swing and his mom's mom awkwardly holding a cat and a cigarette. Ben pastes them to Job and Lamentations, Exodus and Revelation. Ben illustrates his Gideon Index.

THROUGHOUT THE DESERT, Ben sees and ignores signs. POSTED. PRIVATE PROPERTY. KEEP OUT.

Nailed to leaning posts and spelled out on plastic, black and orange. Beyond each sign lie structures collapsed, timbers dry-rotten and broken glass, scoured by sand and by wind. Something discarded and forgotten. But sometimes the signs are different. White sheet metal and block black text. NEVADA TEST SITE or NEVADA PROVING GROUND. An emblem of the Department of Energy. Warnings. Yet the roads are always open. Fused sand and discarded glass. Throughout the desert, Ben sees and ignores the signs.

UP INTO THE GAP he hobbles and disappears. He lets the darkness swallow him whole. He gives himself wholly to whatever's inside.

IN A CROSSROADS town near the Utah border, Ben stops at a clapboard roadhouse. Chases lacquer-hot shots with whatever thin beer foams from the tap. Eats the deep fat-fried whatever that's scrawled on the specials board. Feels immediately like something poisoned beneath a blanketing fallout haze. As soon as he steps through the door, a skeletal woman with blonde puffed hair and a thousand years of barroom nights etched deep into the lines of her face attaches herself to Ben's elbow. Takes up the seat beside him at the bar and launches into an alcoholic monologue. She tells him about her mom and about her cat and asks him to buy her a drink. She tells him how nothing ever happens in this town. She asks him to buy her a drink. Any other night, Ben would take the time to listen, would write down her every word in one of his pocket notebooks. But tonight, the effort is beyond him. With a history of ghost towns and desert highways punctuating the flickering mem-ory of his days—with the promise of countless more ahead—in this moment, all he wants is to be alone. It makes him feel mean, how much he wants to be alone. Again and again, he knocks her pack of menthols off the counter, hoping she'll get the message. When she asks for a white Russian, he orders her bourbon with light cream. He redraws repeatedly the map in his brain to reject her from this room, but her voice and her need recasts her into the roadhouse din and somewhere in her nonsense she mentions a darkroom and a process for transferring negatives to uncommon surfaces—blocks of wood, anything porous—and suddenly Ben is holding her by the shoulders, half-coaxing and half-shaking her, asking if she's a photographer and if her studio is near.

"Near?" And she laughs her halitosis gasp. "Near."

Her laughing in his face is almost too much. He tells her to take him there.

Outside, she leads him through the parking lot and across the empty street, behind a trailer to a bulkhead rising from a bare scratch of lawn. She opens the double doors on screaming hinges, descends the stairs inside. Three-quarter moon and a coyote's howl. Not a breeze. Ben has no choice but to follow her down.

"This used to be a bomb shelter," she says, turning on the one red bulb dangling from the ceiling. "My daddy built it when we was a kid." Her teased blonde hair looks like a bloody mess. "Said it'd someday save us."

The place has been totally gutted. Just a few counters and an industrial sink along one wall, a table with a mechanism that looks like a drill-press, a clothesline strung between the walls for drying prints, the only relic from its shelter-days being a defeated looking Army cot jammed into one corner. Covering the walls, pictures hang, curling at the edges. The woman tries to give Ben the grand tour, show off her work, but he manages to head her off.

"Can you develop these?" he asks, pulling from his pants pocket a handful of spent film canisters.

"I *could*...." A certain hint of sobriety touches the corners of her eyes.

Ben takes his camera from his jacket pocket, pops the release, adds the reel from inside to the collection in his free hand, forces the whole lot onto her. "All these. All of them. Tonight."

"Listen, mister, I don't know who—"

She shuts up as soon as he reaches for his wallet. In the red light, he can barely see which bills are what. "All of them." He hands her what he hopes is about a hundred bucks. "Tonight."

Looks from the cash in his hand to the film in her own. Bites her bottom lip. She probably was pretty once. But that was a long time ago.

"They color," she finally asks, "or black-and-white?"

AND ELSEWHERE, EARLIER or later on, walking the cracked highway shoulder with his Jeep parked far behind, he yells into his cell phone, in the dark and roaring wind, yelling to be heard, "I know, I know, I'm getting closer, but, I don't—fuck, I don't know." But there's no one on the end of the line: in the wind's static howl and the wind of his voice, he hopes they knew enough to hang up.

INSIDE THE GAP, BETWEEN elbow bends carving through the cliff-side rock, Ben kneels on the pebbled floor. Awkwardly fits himself on folded legs. Presses his face into the wall. On his left and right, whisper-thin sunlight leaks into the passage, but where Ben crouches, nose and forehead kissing stone, he sees nothing.

In the black heart of the gap, the darkness swims in to erase all lines, all definitions, and Ben doesn't see a thing. With no borders or divisions, the darkness becomes him, and neither sees a thing.

LIKE A MARIONETTE, clumsily handled and so obviously built of bones, the barfly produces the film, works the developing tank and reel, hangs the wet negatives from her lank clothesline. It occurs to Ben that, to have this space—to gut her father's shelter, to buy and install all the things she needs—this woman must be more than a common drunk with a ten-dollar pawnshop camera. Whatever else she might be or be known as, this is who she is: an artist in secret, hidden alone beneath the ground. Even still, the idea of looking at her pictures right now is a little too much for him. Ben stretches out on the cot propped in the corner and falls into a shallow, restless sleep.

He wakes once to find her beside him, trying to fool with his body. He pushes her away and falls back asleep, and when he wakes again she's back at her station. The wet sound of fingers sluicing through a chemical bath.

"They're almost ready," she says as he sits up. "You're lucky I'm a Samaritan at heart."

He says nothing, doesn't see how her metaphor applies, stands and stretches and begins the slow shuffle around the room, examining each of the tacked-up photos on the wall. Pretty quickly, the theme becomes apparent. In one picture, a grizzled old man—stubbled and partial-plate grinning—stands outside a paint-flaking shack, holding up in one hand the body of a quail that's quite obviously been struck by a car. In another, a little boy with dirt smudging his nose points to the tire-smashed rodent at his feet. In the set of his mouth, the cock of his head: he almost looks proud.

There aren't always people in her pictures. In many, it's just the pressed-flat body, belly ruptured and face frozen in pained surprise as the mysteries inside are revealed in the sun.

"A lot of kids around here help me," she says, coming up behind him. "A couple of the retired fellas, too. People without much but time on their hands. Tell me where they spotted this or that on the road." She puts her hands on his shoulders, her chin on his back.

"Why not take pictures of living things?"

"Who says they're dead?"

He shrugs her off and she backs away. "Your pictures are done." When he turns toward her, her head hangs like a beaten dog's. "They just need a while to dry."

She hands him the negatives in a small envelope—something she was supposed to use to send her electricity payment—and to kill the time, Ben joins her outside while she smokes a cigarette, sits beside her on the bulkhead stoop and watches her sit folded like a locust, hands barely moving to shift the cigarette in and out of her mouth. The night sky overhead is thinning with the faintest hints of blue and day. Stars disappear. The moon's already set. And when this is over, this poor woman will still be here. I will leave, he thinks, and move on and disappear like another day lost to the physics of space and moving bodies, and she will still be here. Hiding in her bunker. Seeking comfort wherever she can. I'll take what I came for and be gone.

At his side, she makes a sound, telling him to take a look. When he turns, she's lifted her shirt up over her belly: on her soft abdominal skin, he can see the crooked ridgeline, the steeply carved canyon face, the twin blind gaps staring out from the stones.

Ben's eyes meet the canyon face's black eyes. But he cannot speak. And he cannot move.

"See what I mean?" she says, touching with the V of her fingers the length of the black gaps. "Any porous surface can be a picture." Rolling her belly, she makes the dead eyes dance. So sad and so beautiful. She rolls her belly, and the dead eyes dance.

In a while when she goes back inside and comes out with his photos in a bulging manila envelope, he gives her another hundred dollars. He hopes she'll maybe use it to get out of this place. If only for a day. If only to the next town over.

Across the street, beside his Jeep all alone in the lot, the roadhouse stands like an empty shack. Something he'd find in Ophir or any other abandoned place. Like something he's been looking for. Ben doesn't look at the pictures until he's far away from this place.

IN HIS MEMORY, HE does not emerge from the gap. That moment is lost to him. As far as Ben knows, he is still kneeling in the dark.

HOW DOES BEN'S short-lived baseball card collection meet its end? One morning a kid in his grade showed up to school with the entire 1981 Topps trading card collection. He didn't have to seek out a single card. He didn't trade or barter. His mother ordered the entire set, factory direct, from a catalogue. And even in this pampered state—all evidence, no work—not one answer was found. Just a box full of inked and glossy paperboard.

After school that afternoon, Ben climbed to a tree limb overlooking the creek and fed his collection to the water below. Everything whisked down and away. Never up. The sun slid behind a cloud.

Upon his homecoming, Ben finds the dusk-lit streets overwhelmed with bodies. Sidewalks teeming, roads closed. Cops standing cow-eyed before their parked cruisers, thumbs hooked through the loops of their belts. He had meant only to pass through on his way to Lundy or Bodie, whichever one he comes to first, or anyway, whichever one exists. But now that he's here among this thronging mob, he decides it might be worthwhile to linger and to see. At first, air so electrified, he thinks there's been an accident. A building collapsing or flashing on fire. But these people are grinning, wide-eyed and laughing, and through this carnival air he finally glimpses a banner strung between street lights—Hot August Nights—and remembers: this is the street fair El told him about, the classic-car show, the sock-hops and doo-wop, everything vintage rolled out for public adoration. One tremendous nostalgia fix. People wander in and out of traffic as if the streets were a parking lot. Cars line up before and behind him and no one seems to move. He abandons the Jeep at the first empty spot he finds.

It's too far to the motel from here, too many people flooding the streets and pushing toward

Virginia where the hot rods and music roar, so Ben ducks into a café with a yellow awning and soap-white pictures drawn onto the glass. A conch shell. A porpoise. A whale. Inside, through the gathered milling bodies, he finds an empty table and orders a Scotch. Breathes in deeply and exhales his claustrophobia. Peels open his envelope of photographs.

Right away it becomes clear to him, these pictures belong in two separate genera. In the first are his pictures of the first Ophir Mill, its crumpled outbuildings, the dark interior of the one he was able to enter. His self-portrait, the picture of his freshly split lip. Ethyl's barely recognizable silhouette in the lounge's vacant gloom. Bear-shredded garbage bags strewn across a lawn. All of these, he examines quickly and sets aside. Because it's the other set of pictures he's interested in. The pictures he doesn't remember taking.

The first picture is of El's house, windows unlit in the deepening light of dusk or dawn, the roof a black imprint against the vaporous sky. Bearing the weight and tone of a threat.

Another picture is of concrete steps leading down to a locked wooden door, almost negligible until he notices the compound-triangle sign nearly outside the picture's frame and, all at once, he recognizes the basement betting parlor. Where he bid on Sparkleberry for Earl. Where he forced Joel down to the floor.

There's a picture of the cliffs at Ophir 2, the twin black gaps staring vacant as a funeral mask. Then another from inside the gap, looking out at the plains and waste, a slim white aperture framed by depthless black.

There are three pictures of the hitchhiker he picked up just outside Carson City. The first shows him stoic and forward facing in the passenger seat, the passing scenery a blur outside his open window. The second is almost a duplication of the first but for the features of the man's face, the bitter twist of lip and tightened brows, eyes like thin black slashes. In the final picture, through the windshield's spotted glass: the figure's retreating form.

There's a picture of Catherine tearful and fists clenched, on the verge of screaming as she stands like a broken spear in the trail above Tahoe. He almost doesn't recognize her for the fury shaping her face. He tries to imagine what he could have said to distill such fury from her. He imagines saying it, then snapping a picture in her face. "No wonder she left me up there."

In another picture, a group of sunbathers gathers around an empty pool. In another, Earl hangs clutchingly from the Jeep's side mirror. His face a fearful clenched fist. The world beyond him a speeding-by blur.

There are more pictures—many more, including one of a Tahoe snow plant unfurling monstrous and alien from leaf-litter humus—but he can't look anymore. The evidence of this other life lived without his knowledge twists like a cold knife in his belly. How much has he done that he cannot remember doing? A shadow version of himself operating while he was not aware. How much did this other Ben choose to not record? What's worse is that these pictures are better. Sleepwalking, he's gathered better evidence than while awake. Ben gathers the pictures in the nest of his arms and lays his head on the table, the sweat on his skin sticking to the resin of the prints, and maybe he falls asleep for a moment but mostly, Ben tries to make his head and heart go blank, and when he feels a presence near him—

something between him and the light trickling over his shoulders and hair, the faint scent of perfume—he thinks it's the waitress coming around to see if he's okay or to maybe kick him out. The last thing he expects to see when he looks up is El sitting down across from him at the table.

"Sorry I'm late," she says, smiling. "What've you got there?"

"Late?"

"I got caught up in traffic." She reaches between his arms, picks up a photo. "Wow. She looks pissed." It's the picture of Catherine on the trail. "Friend of yours?"

"Um."

But she laughs and puts the photograph back with the others, catches the waitress's attention and orders a gin and tonic, sits sipping her drink and playing with the rings of moisture rinking the glass table face, connecting lines of water with her fingertip, and when finally Ben asks her how she knew to find him here, it's her turn now to act surprised.

"I mean, *I* didn't know I was going to be here." He raises his hands off the table, claps them back down. "So how'd you know to come in here looking for me?"

She sets down her drink, looks at him like he's a hurt animal. "Ben"—like a snake eating its own tail—"I invited you here. To have a drink before looking at the cars." She reaches across the table to touch his hand, and he feels simultaneously an urge to jerk away from her and also its opposite, feels a warm burst of comfort rising from where his skin meets hers, traveling up his arm into his spine and skull. He does not remove his hand. "God, Ben, this project must be killing you," and he almost laughs at that, but she's still wearing that worried-mother face that makes everything inside him tighten and hurt and anyway, he doesn't really want to laugh at her. "You should give yourself a little break." He wants to lie alone with her in the darkness of her room. "Try and relax a little." Burrow like a seed into the earth. "Will you promise me that?" But there's no chance of that happening now.

More people are in the café now, flocking in off the street with minds bent toward cherry cokes and vanilla malts. As the resultant noise of voices and glasses swells, a silence descends around El and Ben long enough to assert its presence and when it goes, El asks him, "What can I do to help?"

Because the tone of her voice and set of her eyes are so clearly diminished by the hopelessness of the task—of helping anyone, of ever being helped—Ben has to look away. He sucks his teeth, swirls the ice in his drink. Shuffles through the pictures before him. Dark spaces and tearful eyes. Ghost towns and ghost towns and ghost towns. The closest thing to evidence his research has yielded so far. So concrete and easily destroyed. He thinks of his mangled lip. He thinks of his swollen foot.

Feeding the photographs into their envelope, Ben seals the flap and scrawls a Syracuse address on the front. "You *can* help me." He holds the packet toward her. "Will you mail this for me? First thing tomorrow?"

In the hesitance with which she takes the packet from his hand, he can tell: this is not what she meant by help. Squinting at the address on the envelope, she tries to sound out the name but cannot. "Is this some sort of Odd Fellows lodge or something, Ben, what is this?"

"That's my employer," and he finishes his drink. "They'll be happy to have those." Makes sure the envelope of negatives is still safely tucked in his jacket's inner pocket. "They'll know what they'll be seeing."

El slips the photos into her purse. She doesn't look happy about this arrangement.

"It bothers you," she says, not looking at him, "that I'm so concerned about you."

Ben keeps his hand pressed flat to the table. "I guess I don't see any reason why you should be concerned." It's an effort to not lay it over his face.

"Right." But she still won't look at him. "No reason."

Outside the café, the sidewalk crowd cheers all at once. But Ben cannot see what they're cheering. When the waitress passes by again, El orders them another round, and while they wait for their drinks to arrive, El asks him, "Do you remember the last time you came out here to visit me?"

"Of course." He pauses, fingers the ice in his empty glass. "It was right after—"

"Right. Your parents." El thanks the waitress as she sets down their drinks and leaves. "Do you remember much of what happened on that trip?"

"Um. I think so. I mean, we just screwed around town mostly. As far as I can recall. Went out for a lot of hikes in the desert. Explored the casinos. That sort of thing." Looking past her, he stares at something behind her shoulder, beyond the walls of this room. "I remember, once, we went up to Tahoe and you wanted to take a gondola up the mountainside." He pauses and bites his lip. "I remember going up. I don't remember coming down."

"The gondola." And she smiles. "I remember the gondola."

"But really, that's about it. Nothing to write home about, you know?"

"Are you sure?"

The high-tension wires stretching above the mountain's green trees. The glittering blue diamond of Lake Tahoe down below. And in between, he and El, suspended in sun-white light.

"Yeah. Nothing."

And now she meets his eyes.

"Really?" Reaching across the table, she lays her right hand spread flat against his chest. The corners of her mouth are moving. "Nothing?"

And like a lead sap snapping to the back of his head, mercifully, the darkness closes in.

"SO WHAT STARTED it was, this one *coño* didn't pay me." The girl looks from Ben to the street where shiny cars slowly troll past. She stirs the ice in her cup with her straw. Then she looks back to Ben. "Or he did, but then robbed me once we were done. Fucking *cabron* locked me in the closet and split. You believe that shit? I was in there for, like, an hour before anyone come find me, just naked and screaming. And then I get back to Joey's and have to explain to him what happened. It had to've been about this time of year, right, because Joey was eating this giant fucking peach and he always so fussy about his fruit. Everything got to be in season, you know? So anyway, we in his kitchen and Joey's eating this peach and I'm telling him about this fucker ripping me off. And at first Joey is all calm and shit, just eating his peach and nodding away. Then the next thing I know, he knocking my ass to the floor and smashing that peach of his all up in my face. Like, fucking hard, you know? And it was kinda like rubbing a dog's nose in shit, but it was also like he wanted me to fucking choke on it. Like, stuff it down my throat. But I wouldn't open my mouth. That's how my lip got all cut up here. See? Because of the pit. That's what got me thinking of it, on account of your mouth being all fucked up."

Around them, the crowd moves in its arbitrary tide one way or the other up the sidewalk, some people stopping to stare at the passing cars. Impalas. Phaetons. Chevelles. Ben holds a pocket notebook in his hand, but hasn't written down a word.

"You know, really," she says, abstracted, "it might have been a plum."

"So Joey. He's like, what, your pimp?"

"He my boyfriend, yeah." She takes a sip from her soda. When her fingers touch the straw, he sees painted on her nails: skull faces, blank-eyed and grinning.

"Was that the first time he hurt you?"

Behind him, from among the congress of bodies, he thinks he hears someone call his name.

"Oh shit no! Fucker's hit me lots of times. Probably hit me now if he caught me wasting my time on you." She pokes a long painted nail into his chest and brusquely laughs. Pink lips and green-shadowed eyes. "You know, he even broke my arm one time."

"That must've slowed you down some."

She shrugs, jangling costume jewelry. "You'd be surprised what guys can get into."

"So if your man beats on you so much, why do you stay?"

"Because he's Joey. Why would I want to leave Joey?"

"Because he hurts you? And takes your money?"

She pooches out her lower lip, nods her head from side to side. As if actually considering what he's said.

"Yeah…. But I forgive him."

"How?"

"I just forgive. It's easy, *pendejo*. You just forgive."

"But why?"

"Because I love him."

But to this, Ben only farts through his lips. The girl doesn't seem to notice. She's already turned her attention to a Malibu gutter-roaring down the street while, from the crowd at his back, a hand touches Ben's elbow: El, squeezing past a family of fat kids.

"I thought I'd lost you."

"No such luck." He smiles at her. She smells good. "I had to talk to a friend."

"Her?" El takes his hand and leads him away. "Hopefully not too much of a friend." And she squeezes his fingers, grinning. "When you first got here, you were making googly eyes at pretty teenage waitresses. Now you're hanging out with down-and-out sex workers and refer to them as your friends. You better watch yourself, Ben. You might find yourself at home here after all."

Raising his hands in the air: "*The Helmsman lays it down as law,*" he recites, "*that we must suffer, suffer into truth.*"

"Is that supposed to explain something?"

And Ben drops his hands.

"*Pendejo,*" he says, "means *stupid.*"

El looks at the side of his face, says nothing.

"Everywhere I go, it's what people call me. You were right. Little Mexican kids on bikes? Fucking prostitutes? What the fuck are they seeing, you know?" Then: "I mean, how do they know?"

El opens her mouth to say something. Then she doesn't say anything. Between the sidewalk and the street, low metal barriers keep everyone at parade distance. Glistening hot rods rove the avenue like wolves.

"Your lip looks a lot better now." She presses close to him as they walk, their bodies touching in small ways. Her mouth seems always so close to his. "Much better."

She hasn't noticed yet his limp. Down the side streets, there are vendors and fire-eaters and the collage of too many radios all playing Buddy Holly. She hasn't noticed so much.

THERE ARE SO MANY people walking and standing and staring sheep-eyed at the cars and at the lights, staring drunk—almost all of them drinking, from hidden flasks or big plastic cups—and it seems to Ben that while he was gone roaming the desert heights in search of forgotten places, the city has grown in population, absorbing the peoples of countless smaller towns, inundated with spectators. He had no idea so many people cared about vintage cars, and on one casino wall he sees plastered a banner declaring this to be the biggest classic car show in the nation. So maybe it only seems like a lot of people care, Ben decides, when they're all cloistered together in one tiny place.

Each casino, El explains, hosts its own private exhibit. From the street they enter a casino and walk straight through, past the bustling slots and table games, exit out the back doors into the parking lot where countless silver and cherry red and aquamarine cars stretch and lounge, not one of them younger than fifty years old. People mill and wander, gaping at hood ornaments and polished chrome, the carnival air of the street replaced with something closer to a sober reverence. No one wants to scratch a fender. No accidental flaw in the seamless shining luster.

As they pass between the cars, Ben hears a far-off bullhorn voice echoing from somewhere unseen, statements like bullets with a cheering crowd shouting back.

"When the United States *government* decided it needed a nuclear test site," and the crowd descends into boos, "they decided on the Nevada desert. Because, in *their* estimations, the entire *state* was uninhabitable. But tell me something," and the voice is almost lost in the furious roar. "But tell me something, people: what state do *you* inhabit? What state did your *daddies* inhabit? What state have the *Western Shoshone* inhabited for over *one thousand years?*" And his voice is drowned out by the screams.

"In the past three days," Ben says, "I've been from Elko to Tonopah, and I'd have to say, the U.S. government? They might've been onto something."

"Hey, watch it." El pinches the skin above his elbow and twists. Not enough to hurt. Just enough to let him know that it could. "That's my home you're talking about."

"Just because you live someplace," he says, "doesn't mean you should." He thinks about the towns all along the Mississippi floodplains, in the subtundra of New England and Minnesota, the Dakotas. Every mountainside home hanging above the San Andreas fault. The entire silty bog of Florida waiting for a hurricane to wash it away. And in the face of such unilateral stupidity and doom, he cannot think of anything more useless than gawking admiringly at rank upon rank of ancient, outdated cars.

"So what exactly is the point of this?" he asks, sweeping his hand to take it all in but mostly gesturing to a Tootsie-Pop orange GTO sparkling in the lights.

"I guess it started as a nostalgia thing. Back in the 80s. Sort of a citywide sock hop to bring in some extra summertime tourist dollars." As if to illustrate, she skips a few steps on the pavement. An older man in a fedora stops to watch. "All this stuff with the cars came later. Mostly it was jitterbugs and chocolate malts. I think the Righteous Brothers played that first year."

But Ben shakes his head. "No. I mean, what are *we* doing here? Open-minded as you are, El, you don't really strike me as the kind of girl who goes in for classic cars."

El nods to herself, as if thinking this over. Nearby, two men pop the hood to a turquoise Dodge Coronet and lean in adoringly above the engine. One of them whispers a suspiring "wow" while from unseen speakers somewhere, Santo Farina's slide-guitar rises and falls like the breath of the soundly asleep.

"You're right. The cars aren't that interesting. None of the parts in and of themselves are really all that interesting. But when you consider them all at once, that all these things are happening as part of a singular event and that that event is happening *here*, it paints an amazingly weird scene, don't you think? I mean, this is a uniquely weird city to live in in general. And then, for just a few nights, it *chooses* to be *this*. Like the whole city is lost in some ridiculous, surreal dream someone's grandfather is having. Seriously, doesn't this seem at all strange to you?"

Where the parking lot runs up to the casino gates, a line of girls in matching white blouses and long blue skirts are twirling their hips in circles. Their teeth are shining and lips painted red. Above their heads, a white banner runs:

GUINNESS WORLD RECORD FOR HULA HOOPING BREAKING NOW!

Ben remembers the barfly in the red light of her studio bunker. He remembers El's mouth, touching his for the first time.

"Yes," he agrees, "this all feels pretty strange."

And coming up closer so that he cannot avoid her eyes: "And anyway. It's fun to do things that are new."

He tries to move away from her, step to the side. But she steps to the side with him. Like they're dancing. Almost but not quite touching. While the pretty girls hula-hoop and the waxed Impalas gleam. While the Farina Brothers' guitars dreamily swell. They slow dance to "Sleep Walk" beneath the lights in a casino parking lot.

El keeps her eyes on his eyes. All at once, it's an invitation and a threat. But they're the same thing. The invitation is the threat.

"You know me so well," he says, trying to diffuse whatever she's doing. "I am, after all, all about fun."

Eyes narrowed, she punches his chest and pushes him away. But she's playing. "Yeah. That's you, alright. Doctor Good-Times in the flesh with his Magical Mystery Bag of Fun."

"In fact, this might be too much fun for me. I can hardly stand it. Do you think maybe we could move along somewhere else?"

"I think there's an Elvis impersonator contest over at Circus Circus."

"Um."

"And there's drag racing over at the Nugget. They shut down the whole street for that."

"You're killing me."

"Not yet, I'm not. C'mon, I'll buy you a drink."

Taking his hand, El leads him from among the cars and past the hula hoopers, inside to the casino floor. But among the crush of people—all moving in opposite directions, herding, pressing in—there's nowhere to go, no place to move, so they duck out through a side door that deposits them on a narrow one-way street between a movie theatre and the casino's blind side, and it's like all at once they've stepped into some alternate world, less a car show and more a pagan festival, a pageant for the Day of the Dead. Street lamps shrouded in red, orange, and yellow crepe dance with the light and wind to make a wick of downward flame. Skeletons of bent neon tubes, green and white and red and arranged as a dead mariachi band against one wall, trumpet and fiddle and guitar. Magic lanterns casting shadow dioramas on the street-side walls and onto the street, across the people walking by. A glowing green fog rolling up from the sewer grates, from hidden lamps and smoke machines. A papier-mâché effigy of the president effulgent inside a rusty oil-drum.

Beside him, El grabs his arm. As if she were falling. As if he were a rope.

"It's the Light Show," she breathes, almost inaudible. "I forgot all about this." All around, people seem dazzled, stunned by the sudden remove from the car show, hypnotized by shadows and by the lights. Stooped and misshapen silhouette women performing shadow dances behind a sheet, Mason jars with rubbery mutant bodies floating in green liquid and pale light.

"Every year," El breathes, taking his hand, "different artists present new work. It's completely open-ended, what they're allowed to do. As long as the primary medium is light."

Past them, a parade of grotesques mounted on tall staves marches through the crowd, casting distorted shadow faces on the walls.

"It seems like a lot of folks are doing just the opposite," Ben says. "Manipulating darkness instead of light."

"I'm not sure I see the difference."

Ben pretends to scratch an itch in order to take back his hand.

Where a narrow alley empties onto the street, some people gather in while others shy away. Ben finds himself drawn toward the uneasy crowd. Flanking the alley's mouth, two blindfolded men juggle brands of fire, their flailing throws and near-misses alone keeping many people away. "I wonder what this is about," El whispers. He's certain, she's not aware of the hushed tone she's adopted since stepping out from the casino. Past the jugglers and into the alley's crowd, they weave among the milling bodies until they find, at the alley's dead-end, a clutch of shimmering glass women. Alex's glass women. The swell of hips and cleft of sex. Variously posed and cloistered together to face the surrounding crowd. A barrier chain keeping everyone at least ten feet from the figures, all naked and wearing the same familiar face, and still Ben can't decide: is it peace or fear in their glassy eyes? Is it either? The entire cast is lit by a few bright white spotlights, transparent bodies gleaming icily—there's some sort of gel placed over the lights, projecting an image onto the girls, but he can't tell what it is—but somehow Ben feels that this isn't the light spectacle in its

To Sleep as Animals

entirety. This is prelude, a set stage. Something more is happening.

"They're like the Bouret Venuses," El says. "You know? Like female talismans made for ritual. All slinky and a little bit scared."

And like a puzzle falling into place, Ben recognizes the face.

"A bunch of frightened little girls all carved of melting ice."

Alex's girlfriend from college. The one Alex has been pining for all these years. In duplicate and triplicate, denuded and gathered in a brick and asphalt cul-de-sac. A dead-end. The sort of place anyone could get fucked or get killed.

Somehow, he knows: the gel over the lights is a mushroom cloud. Alex's dreamed-of atomic fire projected onto his girls.

"We should leave," he says. "This isn't going to end well." But before he can move her, a big man in a tuxedo appears, pushing the crowd even further back, calling out in a deep loud voice something about safety, and as the man grabs Ben's shoulders and forces him backward and away from the sculptures, Ben sees and recognizes the tuxedoed man, recognizes Alex all dressed up and shaven yet somehow still a pirate, somehow more so because of his disguise.

"Alex! It's Ben, Alex."

"What's a benalex?" Alex doesn't look at him, keeps pushing back the crowd, sets up another chain between two posts to create a greater physical barrier between the crowd and the glass women. With so many people pressing in from behind to see what will happen next, there's no way they'll escape now. Just like the glass girls: they're trapped. But holding his arm, so bright-eyed and expectant, El won't leave anyway, he knows she will not leave. She wants whatever will happen to happen. She's proud to be so close to it.

Before them, Alex raises one arm over his head and roars into an electric bullhorn, "Ladies and gentleman," but the words hang in the air, everyone waiting for him to say something more as he lowers the bullhorn and disappears into the shadows outside the lights.

With a sizzle, the spotlights go black.

In silence, the crowd holds its breath.

Then the gas jets hiss on.

Ben remembers the deconstructed kiln behind the studio in Boca, remembers Alex's comment, laughing as they drove away. *Now it fires nuclear bombs.* First hidden in the shadows outside the spotlights and now simply hidden—even with their pilot flames lit—it's unclear where and what they are. Once the flames expand and pour forward, what they are no longer matters. Like a half dozen demon tongues, the gas jets lap out over the nearest figures, dance back, then lunge again and do not relent. The glass bodies glow a fiery orange, some burning a fiercer white. As the first features begin to melt and run—noses and chins, fingertips, breasts—a low murmur, disapproving and near panic, builds and ripples through the crowd. But no one moves. Not one person tries to leave. Ben can feel the skin of his scrotum tighten, his insides turning watery. With El at his side, he wishes he were anywhere else. No one tries to move.

When the first glass body explodes, a sound moves through the crowd like a chorus of unified *nos*. When the second and third go, no one says a word. While the bodies nearest the gas jets disintegrate into monstrous hulks, the ones farthest— the ones unevenly lapped by flames, huddled together in the center of the clutch—crack and shatter. The impossible results of hell on human bodies.

Then, with a sudden woof, the jets cut out and darkness floods in, everyone blind and blinking away the sunspot of the flames. When they can see again, a single bright floodlight illuminates the glittering remains, shattered glass sprayed across the pavement in bright fans, the unexploded figures so warped and destroyed, Ben has to look away and when he does, he finds El with her face buried in his shoulder. She doesn't speak when he says her name. She hides her face and shakes against him.

Her name was Colette. He remembers now. Who Alex once loved and then lost so now must lose again in the perpetual horror-show of his memory. Forever doomed to abuse in dark alleys' ends. Her name had been Colette.

Alex, of course, is nowhere to be seen. Eventually, the crowd turns away, files out, and as the last spectators leave, the blindfolded fire-dancers stretch another chain across the alley's mouth. One more place no one's meant to ever see again.

Keeping their backs to the now-cordoned alley, Ben and El drift among the simpler lights of the show—the magic lanterns and silhouette plays—slow and abstracted, as if coaxing their eyes and minds to wander, distracting from what they just saw. For a moment, Ben and El linger again over the neon mariachi band, the clean white light of their skulls, their sombreros' festive yellow and red, and Ben tries to focus on these details—the bend and curve of glass, the almost cosmic glow of spectral colors—tries to erase the memory of Alex's atomic fever dream, its heat and its gravity. It isn't happening. Beside him, El squeezes his hand, a subtle trace of a smile edging at the corners of her mouth as she stares at the skeletal band, and though her eyes still reflect the colored lights with a bright wet sheen, he thinks she looks recovered—or anyway, is recovering, is letting go of what he cannot—and it's as she tugs his hand gently toward the next exhibit and Ben starts to explain that he knows the artist, knows Alex, that she steals the very words from his mouth.

"What?"

"We went on a date once." She gazes at a model living room set up along a brick wall to their left, a couch and end table with a softly glowing lamp. "Just once. It wasn't very fun." The body of the lamp is a woman's upraised arm. Its shade hides the bulb in her hand. "All he wanted to talk about were nuclear bombs. Seriously. Not the obvious stuff, you know, like their military use—his stance on *that*, I remember him saying, was that by the time Hiroshima and Nagasaki rolled around, it was already too late. No, what he really seemed fixated on were the nuclear test sites, these huge unspoiled stretches of Nevada desert, or later on when they were setting off bombs under the ocean or over Bikini Atoll. He couldn't get over it, how it was like we were going out of our way to find the most beautiful, remote places in the world just to destroy them the most horrible way we knew how." El stops to pull the lamp's chain. Turns off its light. Turns it back on. "That's what he was obsessed with, that we *chose* to do these things, and when we witnessed the results, we weren't disgusted or ashamed but kind of turned on by it. This is what this jackass wanted to talk about throughout the date! This was his idea of seductive. We blew up the best the world had to offer, and it got us off. So we kept doing it, again and again, just blowing up the desert, blowing up the ocean. Setting the sky on fire. And he kept using this phrase—you know how drunks are, they just repeat things—he kept saying, 'Once we donned the executioner's hood, we found we loved it and refused to take it off.'" Leaning in toward him, still holding his hand, El meets Ben's eyes and smiles conspiratorially. "By the looks of things, his stance on the matter hasn't much changed, huh?"

"Wait. But how did you guys meet?" He knows he's missing the point. There's something else he doesn't want to miss.

"Like I said, on a date. That was the first time we met."

Ahead, beyond the crowd: the throaty roar of an engine. Menacing and sexual in the heavy August air.

"So, what, someone set you two up?"

"No. It was a date. Through a service." And for the first time, Ben hears the quotes around the word "date." All around him the lights shine as one single white blur. By his hand, El is leading him back toward the street. "Like I said. It's fun to try out new things." Then she adds, feeling him bristle, "It's not like I've been waiting around for you my whole life, Ben."

He shakes his head, confused. "You're losing me, El."

And now she's the one shaking her head. "That's the problem," she says, and he knows, all at once, the subject has changed. "It's the one thing you can't accept. You'll never lose me, Ben. You can't. This isn't that kind of game. And I'm not losing you, either. It's the one thing that isn't allowed. And you keep looking for an exception to the rule."

And like the flash in the sky that tells it's too late, it strikes Ben, the nuclear flash of the truth. She loves him. The only person in this whole dried-out world defined by ghost towns and graveyards, everything built by people who loved and then left. His open desert. His Bikini Atoll. She loves him. And what's worse: he loves her back.

From the light show, they push through the crowd back onto Virginia, where the air is open and the hot rods thunder like gods prowling along the tar. They stop and stare at the passing cars, letting this moment be their conversation's conclusive punctuation, and in a minute, El tells Ben that she has to use the bathroom, she'll be right back, wait right here. And as she dashes inside the Eldorado, Ben stands and lets the night air swirl around him, the passing crowds swirl around him, the scent of octane and fried dough and spilled beer and powdered sugar swirl around him and at some point the whirlwind of his senses spins out and away as the gathered bodies briefly part and across the street, standing on the corner beneath the Silver Legacy's flashing neon marquee, Ben sees Zack the grey boy standing with a taped-up suitcase and a clean grey sports coat. His hair is combed and slicked back against his skull. His beard is trimmed. Ben bets his nails are clean, too. He crosses the street and says hello to the grey boy, the grey boy no more.

"Mister Ben." Zack smiles without showing his teeth, takes Ben's hand, shakes firmly. Like office mates. All business. "I thought you'd split for good."

"Not yet." Ben takes back his hand. "You look spruced up." Glasses clean, tusks absent from his ears: in his cleanliness, he looks diminished, stripped of himself.

"Fall semester's coming up. Gotta head back." And almost sheepishly, he adds, "The summer's phantasmagoria is ended."

Ben laughs, "Of course, absolutely, I suppose for you it is," and Zack gestures toward the parading cars on Virginia, the whitewalls and cherrybomb exhausts.

"My dad's driving one of the cars in the show. When this is over, we're riding back to Piedmont in a '76 Ranchero."

And again, Ben laughs, shakes his head but moves his hands in such strange ways, not knowing what to do with them. "Shit kid, I knew you were too good to just give it all up."

There's a humorless edge, the way Zack smiles. "What are you getting at, man?"

"You, Zack. You had me going for a while, I thought you'd really bought into the lifestyle. Were an apprentice grey man."

"Grey man?"

"Earl's little protégé."

The smile, even a false one, is gone now. "You don't get it, do you?"

"Sure I get it. You were slumming for the summer. Now it's back to school for you. I'm sure you'll get a great paper out of this. B+ material, for sure."

Out in the street, an engine guns and roars in a pageant of itself. Voices shout approval. Zack shakes his head and looks away. "Whatever, man. You've clearly got your own agenda here."

It's a blanket thrown over him, the way the urge to sleep comes on. Like a sudden dark wave trying to pull him under. He has to fight to keep above its tide.

"Yeah, whatever. A solid response. Listen: have you seen Earl?"

And like a glass slipping in slow motion from a table, spilling in a mercury arc, he feels the moment skidding out of his control. A trio of biker-types pours out of the Silver Legacy in their leather and beards just as Zack turns to dash between them toward the casino's doors, aiming to put their bodies between himself and Ben. But before Zack can get away, Ben reaches out to grab the taped-up suitcase, and like yanking a ripcord, he pulls the kid back. Stumbling, Zack shouts and goes down, hits the sidewalk hard, his jacket ripped and elbow bleeding. Ben descends over him like a striking snake, but before he can do much more than twist his fists around the collar of Zack's shirt, two hands close over Ben's shoulders and yank him up and away from the grey boy, and first someone shouts what the fuck is going on and then no one is shouting anything because there's a gun in Ben's hand and his gun's black eye is looking one of the biker's in the face, at a spot just under the man's left eye where his cheek disappears into his beard, and as the moment resolves to crystallize in Ben's mind, he sees it for what it is and sees how wrong he has become.

Amid a frozen crowd of a thousand people, he holds his gun in a stranger's face. He waits in the stillness for anything to stop him. At his feet, Zack lies bleeding on the pavement. Around him, no one moves. Even the engines' blats are muted. He cocks the hammer with a resigned click. Disgusted, the biker looks away.

It's in this moment of unilateral disapproval that Ben sees El step out of the Eldorado. Look around for him and finally see him. The shock as she actually *sees* him. It makes him wither, the stunned-sick way she looks at him. His one ally in all the world agrees with everyone else. He's wrong. Gun quavering in his hand: with her watching, he knows he cannot do this.

He shrugs a lame apology to the bikers and to Zack, to everyone with their eyes trained on him. He stuffs the pistol between his belt and back. He feels the weight of who he is crushing like a great hand from above.

Above the crowd, a single voice rises to shout the one word of Spanish he has learned.

Ben runs.

IN FLASHES OF LIGHT peppered mercifully with darkness—street lights and casino lights, the faces of strangers disgusted or ambivalent, a band on a stage playing Chuck Berry songs and the sudden crash as he rolls across the hood of a bubblegum pink Bonneville—Ben runs until he reaches the park near the river, almost cries in relief when he finds the place empty. The entire city confined to ten crowded blocks. Everywhere else is deserted. Crossing the park's wide sloping lawn, he slides down the embankment into the Truckee River, wades for a ways through the shallow wash, then hides in the shadows beneath a bridge. It's a while before he realizes that no one is chasing him. In a town teeming with drunks and prostitutes, pimps wielding knives and ten thousand strangers from out of town gilded to the hilt with expense and glamour, all so ready to steal and be stolen from, to be killed or make a killing: Ben's outburst barely blipped on the radar.

Hunkered in the shadows near the river, Ben wonders if it's maybe time he retire from the world of people. Return to the desert's dry kiss, to the ghost town he's yet to find. Crawling out from under the bridge, Ben keeps to the vacant streets, far from the lights and music and voices. He finds his Jeep and keys inside. Starts the engine. Heads south.

Somewhere in this desert, he thinks, there is a ghost town not on any map. Its name is Bodie or its name is Lundy. It hides somewhere near the salted banks of Mono Lake. Merging onto 395 on the south side of the city, rushing through the night in the rattle of his Jeep, he's certain: it is waiting.

Chapter 10

THE JEEP WAVERS between lanes for a while. Then it slips off the road to the gravel. Gliding fast off the highway and down an embankment into a wide concrete culvert. When the force of impact shakes Ben awake, the Jeep is rising up over the culvert's far lip, up and over but at an angle so that when the Jeep detaches itself from the earth and is airborne, it takes on a corkscrew twirl and lands unevenly on its roof, carves a deep gouge in the ground as it slides, eventually comes to rest on its crumpled passenger side though in the dark, Ben sees none of this. He awakes and the headlights are pointing at culvert cement, then the vague nothing of night sky, then are smashed out as he lands.

For a long time, he lets his seatbelt hold him hanging. Nose bleeding and split lip reopened. The ache across the bridge of his nose where the steering wheel smacked his face tells Ben he'll probably have a matching set of black eyes by morning. Otherwise, everything feels fine. His bones are still bones. His lungs are still lungs. Nothing punctured or shattered or split. Ben feels like he's made out okay.

Wriggling out from his seatbelt, Ben drops down in a graceless crouch on the new floor of the passenger side door, takes stock of what he has in the Jeep, what he needs to carry from here, what can be left behind. There are notes scattered all around the cab, things that haven't yet been absorbed into the greater body of research in his room at the 777, things yet to be compiled into his Gideon Index. But at this point, it looks unlikely that he'll ever return to his motel. And that's okay. Not going back is okay. As long as he keeps moving forward, he can leave the rest of this behind, his notes and his map and his list of lost places. He can leave what he doesn't need behind. Loading his last of roll of film into his camera, Ben drops the empty canister among the other refuse and crawls out of the wreckage. No longer his Jeep, just a Jeep. Something else smashed up and lost along the highway.

Through the night, Ben keeps to this side of the culvert, keeps out of the passing cars' lights. For the moment, he does not want to hitch a ride. He does not want to be seen.

BY DAWN, HE FINDS himself in Carson City. Strip malls and divided streets. A generic nowhere. The sort of place most everyone could have come from.

He wants to eat but doesn't. His bowels are heavy but with what, he can't imagine. He cannot remember the last time he ate. After wandering some time among identical blocks of franchise hamburger joints and chain electronics stores, Ben finds the bus depot, through the dirty glass doors heads straight for the public bathrooms, and as he's cleaning up at the sink, he sees himself in the greasy mirror and experiences the sudden lurching vertigo of a stereogram puzzle revealing itself to crossed eyes. Mouth torn and crusted black with old blood, swollen and pink with fresh blood and pus. Lips chapped and peeling. Sunken eyes dark with more than just bruises. The pale eggshell of scalp peeking through thinning hair. He looks like a cancer patient after his first dose of chemo. He looks irradiated. But what's worst is the leering grin these features coalesce to assemble.

Ben cleans himself up the best he can. Keeps the tap running so the sink steams and the water is disinfecting hot. Rubs liquid soap into his stubble and thinning hair, inside his crusted-shut nostrils, against his loose and filthy teeth. When he's done, he looks better—still damaged, but less insane—and a few minutes later, at the ticket counter with pink-scrubbed skin and the dust pounded from his jacket, he buys himself passage to Mono City and the agent doesn't blink once at him, says "please" and "sir," and Ben knows his disguise has worked.

THE TICKET AT LEAST solves one mystery for him.

MONO CITY, CA

He was looking at the wrong map all along.

The Greyhound meanders down the southern highway, stopping every few miles to pick up or drop off people in Dresslerville and Walker and Sonora Junction, crossing the border into California with no nod or notice and the entire way, Ben sleeps in the back-most seat, curled up with his head against the window, sleeps without waking for any rev or brake, sleeps through his stop and dreams.

In one, he is swimming in a river, the white sun above turning the water to silver, cool and clean. Someone else splashes nearby and there are many someones all around, a yellow dog paddling in panting loops around him, among them. Though he feels it's near, he cannot touch bottom. Though he feels it's near, he can't see either shore.

In one, he stands without a shadow on the banks of a great salt lake. Beach rimed white and dead fish drifting at the water's edge, glittering in reeking piles. The air a sulfurous haze with a mountain of fire burning—screaming—at his back while something wet clings tightly over his face. But in another dream, he and El walk along the reservoir canal, holding hands as the wind blows through them, filling their lungs with laughter, and they become the air.

When the bus stops in Crestview and the driver kicks him off, it takes Ben a while to realize he's not in Mono City. No lake. Just a lot of trees and red pine straw underfoot. Working the registers at a nearby gas station, a girl with a T-shirt declaring herself a future MILF clues him in to the mistake he's made, and heading north now up 395, thumb out, Ben walks backward along the shoulder, heading back the way he came.

ONLY ONE CAR PULLS over for him. A busted-up red pickup with a smashed-in grill and Bondo comprising one entire rear fender. It gets him most of the way. Through Ponderosas thinning to stone and brush and baked earth and dust. It's the only ride he needs.

"Heading to Mono, huh?" The driver is florescent with sunburn, a white peel of dead skin cropping up along where his cap chafes against his bristled, rubbery neck. "Pretty interesting place, that Mono." He says the name like it's two separate words: Mo No. He speaks like he's afraid to show his teeth. "Big old salty lake of poison, that one is." And when Ben fails to respond: "That's where the Dodo bird went extinct, you know? When people talk about the Dodo's last stand? They talking about Mono."

Outside, the sun cuts clean through the blue of the sky, carves into the baked brown earth, the black of the road, the western mountain teeth. Purifying. The wind scours. "You don't say."

"Yessir. They lived on an island, see, out in the middle of the lake, and where they had no natural predators, they was a mellow bird. Pretty near domest'cated theyselves." The man lights a half-burnt cigarette from the overflowing gullet of the dashboard ashtray, works up gusty clouds of stale smoke. A putrid smell. He does not open his window. "But then one year," and he exhales, "they's a drought, see, and the water level in the lake went way the fuck down. So low, in fact, that they's something like a bridge in some places, running from the shore to the island. Not much of a bridge, you know, but enough for the coyotes to run 'cross. Damn birds sat and watched they own selves get eaten."

Outside, the truck passes rumbling along a concrete overpass above a bone-dry creek.

"The Dodo," Ben says when he's sure the man is done, "were on Mauritius. Their eggs were eaten by pigs."

For a long time, the man doesn't say anything. Smokes his dried-up crust of cigarette down to the filter. Stabs out the ash. As the miles roll silently by, Ben settles deeper in the bench seat and sleeps. But each time, before too long, the driver nudges him awake, jerks the wheel, hits the brakes. Even once simply saying, "Wake up, white boy" in a drawl Ben notes is flattening, is dangerously wide.

"Before I forget," Ben says, lowering his head to the dashboard's vent, "I'd like to thank you for picking me up. My name is Ben Nigra, from Syracuse, New York, and though I don't say it to be rude, it doesn't really matter what your name might be. Unless I write them down, I usually forget names. Then feel guilty for forgetting. And I don't have any notebooks anymore. So please, don't tell me your name."

The truck passes by a gas station that looks as though entire presidential administrations have come and gone since it last opened for business.

Pumps like rusted robots. A sign so smashed as to mean nearly nothing: a shattered I, a shattered O.

"Now it seems to me that you're requiring some interaction, some social currency. Talking. So before I forget, I need to tell you something. It might explain something about," and he waves a hand to take in his ruined clothes, his blackened eyes, his ripped-apart mouth. He means it to encompass much more. "Back when I was in college, I had this girl I would sometimes visit. We weren't in love, and as far as lovers go, we weren't much to speak of, either. We'd meet. We'd fuck. We'd sometimes hang around her apartment afterward, not really saying or doing much until one of us finally decided to leave. This girl had a cat and one day when the girl left and I didn't, I sat there and watched her cat. It didn't do a whole lot, and it certainly didn't regard me much at all. It ate. It cleaned itself. It walked around. But mostly it slept. It would sleep and wake to lick its foot or get a drink and then it'd sleep again. Its sleep was a faucet the cat could just turn on or turn off. It slept until something better needed to be done, until the girl came home. Then the cat rolled around on the floor and purred and the girl played with the cat and neither one of them needed to fall asleep. I eventually went home."

"Listen mister, I—"

"Shhh…." Ben holds a finger to his lips. "I'm getting to it. See, I thought about that a lot. About the cat and its sleeping. About all animals sleeping. Not as a huge portion of each day. But in the dead spaces. While waiting. When they might as well not be alive. I'd think of animals sleeping when I was on the train or standing in line somewhere, any time I was waiting, wherever people wait. And I saw my life dwindling away while I waited.

"So I developed a method. I taught myself to sleep as an animal. To erase the most pointless moments of my life and feel healthier for it. Refreshed. I eventually mastered my method. I hardly slept at night. I could live multiple lives at different levels of my city, a life in the dark and a life in the day, and in the wasteworks of buses or lobbies or tedious ticking minutes, I slept. But now—and this is the important part—now I'm afraid my method has mastered me. I think my waking selves and sleeping selves are vying for control, and no matter who wins, I will be the one to lose. Because someone has to do the waiting. Someone has to get you where you're going."

The driver keeps biting his lips. Tongue flicking between his teeth. Finally says, though as no sort of response, "Listen: no one rides for free."

It's only then that Ben sees the open fly in the man's stained denim lap, the tortured-red penis peering between unzippered teeth.

Tires whumping against tar. The heavy puff and whistle of flaring nostrils. An incident of bodies in space. Drawn together, pulled apart. Whether he means to or not, Ben laughs, low and quiet at first then bubbling from his belly, hurting his ribs, now not so quiet, not low at all, and when the driver moves toward him—rushes, in fact, in a sideways tackle—it takes Ben a moment to realize what's going on. Not so much a passionate lunge as a hand flapping at the door's handle and lock, an elbow in his chest, and Ben figures it out. He swats the hand away from the lock. He punches the driver's soft belly, and for a second they're both back in their former places and Ben thinks it's over, but the driver is simply correcting their course, keeping the truck on the road, and a moment later he's on Ben again, driving his fists into Ben's empty stomach, his washboard ribs, and as Ben's door clicks and swings open, the wind a howling bite beside him as the driver attacks the seatbelt's buckle, Ben sees the geometry of the moment align, sees himself moving through the angles and lines, reaching one hand past the driver to grab hold of the wheel, turn it hard to the right while his other hand punches the airbag to deploy and suddenly, there are no hands on him anymore. The cushion inflates with a shotgun blast, smashing against the driver's sidelong body, forcing him up against the seat and back window, but by the time the truck hits the guardrail and starts down the steep ravine, the airbag's not doing much more than getting tangled and bloodied as the truck drops down and punches nose-first into the ground. The fat man's body crumbles against the steering wheel, hair showered in broken glass, his breath a flapping wet rag. The truck balances on its nose for a second, then drops back onto its wheels with a crunching bounce, steam hissing from the crumpled hood. Limp and rag-dollish but for the blood pouring from everything, the man slides down to a kneel on the cab's floor, bent backward and sprawling on the seat. Ben unlatches his seatbelt, kicks open his door, gets out.

His head is spinning and hurts in a dull yet tremendous way. He pukes in the dust and nearly falls but keeps himself upright, keeps moving, feet snarling in the dirt, and as his head clears he redirects himself, keeps a course safely distant from the highway, stumbling and trying to control his breath. Chances are good that he's broken a rib. When he can no longer see the wreck over his shoulder, Ben calls 911 and reports seeing a truck drive off the road.

"I'm on a bus heading south. I saw it from out the window."

He waits for the sirens to come and go, waits and again, they come and go. He kicks his way through the sparse brush back to the highway. He hurts but knows he looks okay: no new blood or bruises. Just pain. Just shaking. He keeps to the highway's rough shoulder and listens for the approach of cars. But by then, the lake is just over the next ridge. A sparkling green body of salt. He's almost there.

Douglas W. Milliken

Below the lake, in a garage off the highway just south of the town of Lee Vining, Ben tries to explain what he's doing, where he's looking for, and the black man behind the counter—filling out orders when Ben walks in, sipping a can of orange soda with a straw while a hand-rolled cigarette smolders from the corner of his mouth—listens patiently to his associative ramble. When Ben's verbal flood bubbles to a stop, the black man lays his pink palms to the countertop, puffs his smoke, and tells him, "It sounds like you're getting two different places confused here, son, and there ain't one thing I can do to untangle that mess for you. There is a Lundy nearby, and there is a Bodie. As far as I know, neither one has what you'd classically call a population, but as far as fires and prostitutes chasing trains, that's all news to me." Using his finger as a pen and the countertop as a page, the black man draws a map for Ben. "We're here. Lundy's over here to the northwest, Bodie's over here to the east and a bit further north. Neither one's near much of anything, so you're not likely to be hitching a ride there. You're going to have to walk. Now, I have a boy here, Noah, who's heading up to Bridgeport to pick up some parts from the NAPA there, he's leaving in about twenty minutes. You could ride with him until here"—and he taps one point on the invisible map—"or here"—taps again—"depending on where you decide to go. But I'm afraid that's about the best I can do for you."

Ben shakes the man's callused hand, notes the name-patch sown into the breast of his grease-stained coveralls: CLIVE. "Thank you, Clive."

"Clive worked here before me," and when he smiles, his teeth are yellow bones. "I was a perfect fit."

NOAH IS A SHORT AND bearded grinning young man. The fact that the patch on his coveralls corresponds to the name Ben's been told fills him with a sense of unease.

Because so far Bodie and Lundy have been interchangeable, Ben tells him he's headed to Lundy. When the kid gets in the truck and starts the engine, Ben hauls himself lamely into the pickup's bed.

"No offense, kid." He leans around the edge to speak in through the open window. "I've had some bad luck on the inside of vehicles lately. If it's all the same to you, I'd just assume I stay back here."

"Oh, hey, whatever dude," and Noah grins. "I mean, it's your haircut we're talking about."

Ben lies down in the bed between a spare tire and a busted muffler. He watches the blue vault of sky pass flawlessly overhead. No clouds to break up the view. Nothing to interrupt the passing. Perfection. Ben remains awake the entire ride.

TIRES SNARLING FROM pavement to gravel, Noah pulls to the shoulder at the intersection of two roads, flags his arm out the window and twice slaps his door. As Ben drops carefully down off the truck, he can see—one busted road tumbling westward into the mountains, one squirreling through fields into the north—this isn't the drop-off the false-Clive marked on his invisible countertop map. Noah took a detour.

Pointing up the westward road: "That way to Lundy, huh?"

"Yeah, man."

Squinting at the faint line of 395 to the east, Ben would have to guess: easily four or five miles shaved off his hike. Standing where the two roads meet, Ben thanks the kid for the ride.

"Yeah, sure, well, *vaya con Dios, pendejo.*" His smile seems so permanent and true. "Good luck finding your shit."

"Thank you."

The truck pulls off the shoulder, eases onto the road, ascends gears, is gone.

THE ROAD STARTS STEEP but levels out. Then it gets steep again. Between gusts rolling down the grade, the midday heat is amazing. Far off over the farthest ghostly Sierra peaks, the first traces of clouds are surfacing, huge and black but so far, still far away. No cars have passed him. He hasn't seen a single sign. His left foot is an anchor and his heart is a chain. Ben plods up the mountain road.

Eventually, the pavement cracks and crumbles. Alongside the road, birds watch him from the tangled boughs of crippled trees, doomsday trees, this is the land that fire forsook and even the birds know it.

Ben tries to ignore his left ankle. His left ankle will not be ignored. Eventually the cracked pavement gives way to dust.

HE REMEMBERS HOW, when they were kids, they would wrestle furiously for the first few days of any visit. Play king of the mountain even when the ground was flat. Every leg-race ending in knotted limbs. And El was always the aggressor. Two years younger and half a head taller. He was so glad she was the aggressor.

And after those first few days, when they'd finally gotten it out of their system, they could walk together in the woods or in the foothills, wherever they were, they would swim in any creek, leave their clothes on the shore, hang half-naked and drip-drying from a tree. And he would tell her how he created their grandmother with the egg of his seed. How even the sun could not defy the kiss and fist of gravity. He'd tell her all the things he could not tell anyone else and not once did she ever turn away. She listened to the secrets that defined him and define him still. El never turned away.

CHANCES ARE VERY high, he tells himself, that I could die up here. Two miles in—the wind has stopped, the earth's a brick oven—Ben folds himself into the thin shade of a dead tree. A gnarled skeleton hand reaching out from the dust toward the sky. Buried alive on the road to Lundy.

"This was a really good idea!" he almost shouts, and somewhere a crow lights off from a treetop, laughing with each wing beat. His left ankle keeps throbbing the same one-note song. It's killing him. "When they find me," he tells it, "you'll be the one who gets the axe." But his ankle keeps singing its song.

Under the sun's watchful eye, a narrow black snake works its way across the road, away from Ben, toward whatever it is that snakes side-wind to reach.

"It seems pretty clear now," he tells its retreating line, "that I probably killed my homeless friend." The snake doesn't listen, is slithering, is gone. "For no good reason." Not even a writhing trail in the dust. "Men dressed as women." Somewhere, the crow laughs and laughs.

A pebble skittering down the hillside. A dead leaf rattling to itself. Struggling to his feet, Ben hobbles further up the road toward Lundy.

To his right the ground slopes up toward some indistinct peak, stones like smashed dinner plates litter and pile, narrow little conifers battle up from the dried-up dusty soil. To his left the earth drops like a bucket in a well and all the trees are leafless, bone-ash and grey, and somewhere deep down there runs a creek with no water. On this ruined stretch of empty road, Ben puts one twisted foot in front of the other, drags himself toward Lundy.

I will not find what I'm looking for. He's not sure if he's speaking or thinking. I will probably die today.

He pushes on another mile. Over the peaks, the clouds approach. To fill and flex darkly to the west. The sun is a compass point straight overhead, an accusing finger, a spotlight. The road drops and bends and around the bend the road forks, one up and one down, but the road slanting to descend the slope wears an orange sign at its mouth, saying something about a dam, saying not to enter, so Ben pushes on and a half-mile more along the upper road, a gate crosses his path and he has no choice but to stop. Just a bar on a hinge between two posts. Easy to open. Easy to bypass on foot. But in a quick rundown, Ben does the mathematics—wrecked two cars, maybe killed two men, pulled a gun in a crowded city street with over a thousand witnesses, almost all in the course of 24 hours—and though this seems so minor an infraction, he knows that this is a bad idea. Nothing good can come from his crossing this gate. His luck will soon leave him. His path to Lundy ends here.

Dropping to his knees in the road before the gate, Ben takes off his jacket, puts it back on. Scoops up a handful of dust and rubs it in his hair. Across his face. Into the sweat of his neck. The gummy spit of his tongue. Somewhere beyond the gate, Lundy lies in ruin. Houses burnt out. A church caved in and half-buried under the weight of a mountain's sliding face. Everything someone worked so hard for. Destroyed and abandoned and forgotten.

A cool wind blows the dust from his hair. The clack of dead branches coming together, falling apart. Don the mask and erase the blackboard. Reset everything to zero. Ben pulls the pistol from his belt. Examines its lines, its minor heft and plastic sheen. Throws it down the ravine. He takes out his camera and sets it on the ground. Aims its lens away from Lundy, down the path he has already come.

"If this is the culmination of my search," he says, "then let this be my evidence."

We forgive to wipe clean the stain of transgression. We transgress to be free from the burden of forgiveness. *The Helmsman lays it down as law.* We transgress to be free.

He programs the camera to flash off once every thirty seconds. He finds his feet and stands looming above the camera. Like a cocking hammer: *click*. He turns his back on Lundy and the approaching black clouds above the mountains. He turns toward what he's been running from all along. The camera flashes and he sees it now, the magic mirror, his shadow's cell, the mask he's worn and that has protected him. He sees himself as he is, as from his camera—flashing, winding—he recedes and disappears.

Chapter 0

Ben catches the next flight out, and is gone. He does not go back to the 777. Does not collect his Gideon Index. Walking along the airport highway, the road and the rain just sort of pass through him: he does not put out his thumb for a ride, arrives at the gates drenched in colorless mud. Buys his ticket and drifts through security and in an hour, is gone. No one speaks as he passes through.

And he does not sleep on the plane. He does not eat or drink. He stares at the back of the headrest in front of him. Passengers sneaking wary glances—among tired moms and retirees and young men with fraternity rings who lost more on the floors than they gained, this singular wet and shell-shocked man—but he cannot care about these people. Outside his window, the whole world lies hidden beneath one great grey cloud, containing all horizons. Frames of darkness. Frames of light.

There's a five-hour layover between connections in Minneapolis. Empty-handed, Ben wanders the wings of each terminal and the airport's central hub of mall—food courts and newsstands and automated massaging chairs—but does not remember ever being here before, his memory from just weeks ago long gone. Near a vendor selling hamburgers, Ben finds a bench and sits, a squat cement planter at his back bursting with rubbery banana leaves: they stretch above and hang over his shoulders, dark green with purple bands. He watches the hungry people come for hamburgers, tired people, waiting people. He stretches himself out on the bench and closes his eyes.

Through the PA system, a voice echoes out through the airport mall, howls up into the rafters. Ben opens and closes his eyes. Breathes the scent of meat cooking. He knows people are looking: let them look. Opens and closes his eyes.

To get from Lundy back to the city, Ben only needs three rides. An Indian in a cargo van. A Mexican farmer with a pickup. A Mormon housewife and her worried hatchback. The radio's static hum. Everyone silent inside. By the time the last ride brings him into the city, the clouds off the mountains have gathered deeply. Iron at the edges but black at the heart. He gets dropped off at Virginia and Plumb—in a motel parking lot next to a Chinese diner—and as Ben heads west, amid the thinning streets and thunderhead dusk, the first drops of rain start to fall. Earth so dry the water beads on the ground, little pearls skinned in dust. But soon enough, the ground is helpless but to swallow.

Caught in the year's first rain, Ben walks the sizzling blacktop to his cousin's house. Ruined clothes plastered to his skin, lashed by wind, bleeding dust and sweat and crusted red-brown stains. Ben walks to El's house through the rain.

The door is wide open when he arrives. The house a dark sleeping eye and El kneeling on the floor between the kitchen and the living room, kneeling in a pale cotton dress amid a mess of dropped papers, awash in the storm's swath of grey light. She gathers the papers and sees Ben and jumps, drops the papers again, is expecting no one today, now, in a storm, so jumps when she sees Ben standing like a pillar of salt in her doorway.

She tells him to come in, to dry off. Tells him she opened the door and windows to let in the cool storm air, the sweet perfume of wet earth, wet grass. The outside wind blows around them inside, spiraling and misted while the rain growls into the ground. El tells him he looks worn out, run thin. Her concern is a widow's veil. She does not mention last night. She tells him to please come in.

Ben does not come in. He stands in the vacant doorway wearing the storm-light as a mantle, and by the way El squints at him, shielding her eyes with one hand, he can tell he is hard to see. A dark shape in a storm-bright gap. The light makes him hard to see. The dark makes him hard to see.

If history is of any relevance, the storm over Syracuse when Ben arrives early the next morning is the same storm as when he left. It'll be here when he's gone for good. Washing grey mud down the streets. Someone waiting at the airport to take him home. His studio apartment cool and ghostly with his absence. No light but the storm light through the windows. The scent of dust and the scent he's brought with him, the scent of desert and sweat and the scent of El—her blood and her sex—still clinging to him under his clothes. His mouth hurts. Am I sleepwalking or awake? I'm awake. His ankle hurts, too. I'm dreaming I'm awake. I'm awake. He goes into the bathroom to wash his desert evidence away.

The echo of a voice sounding from the PA, someone speaking who he'll never see. How much of my life is unseen? He stitches shut the cut in his lip with a sewing needle and thread. Stares at his reflection in the mirror. Which side of this thing am I on? In his reflection, in the yellow bathroom light, his shadow casts across the wall. Which side?

Ben sits up on the bench and rubs his eyes. Watches people approaching the stand. He still has hours to wait. He'd buy a burger if he had any money. He spent his last dollars on escape. He lies back on the bench beneath the umbrella of rubbery leaves, watches them nod and wave. Up above him, where the echoes gather, a skylight reveals a clear blue sky. But I thought it was raining. He blinks at the blue light. I thought it was night.

Rolling over to press his cheek into the cool metal bench seat, Ben thinks of how everything seems so far away—the branch above the river, El's laughter skating away in the wind—thinks of Hanover shouting at him in the wastes of Ophir Mill. *If they really wanted it so bad, they'd still have it.* But it's never so simple as that. Because what you want most is what you can never have: you are mandated, it's your job not to have it. You leave what you love because you love it. Pour mercury in the water. Choke your girlfriend with a peach pit or build her out of glass so you can break her. Take the next flight out and get gone.

El puts her reordered papers down on the floor and goes to get him a towel, and when she returns and asks him again, this time, he comes in. He does not take the towel. He does not try to speak. He wants to tell her that he's sorry, he's so tired, he wants so badly to be shut of this, he's tired. He wants his shadow back, he means to say. He wants out of this mask and mirror. He means to say this but doesn't. Because he wants, he cannot. Because this is not his game to play. He is only a vessel. And this point he does manage to convey.

"What?" Her voice is a cloud funneling up toward the sun. "What did you just say?" But he does not say it again. He grabs her and pushes her toward the floor, pushes and she stumbles but still stands so he pushes her again and this time she staggers and slips on her papers and she goes down hard on her shoulder, almost on her neck—the pained sound that escapes her is wrenching, almost makes him stop—and though she tries to get up, he's on her and pushing, pinned over her and pushing, across the floor they're squirming and he shakes her, her head bangs hard off the floor and he pushes again and her eyes meet his and he pushes, he sees her fear and confusion and something more, even as she fights back there is something else, a tenderness, an unwillingness to hurt him, a grasping at wrists and ribs, under his arms—she's trying to tickle him—because this could be a game, this could still be a game for her, not attacking and not trying to stop him, just change the approach, the tone, the accent: her eyes don't plead but insist and her fingers insist and bit-thin lips insist as he pushes and tears at her dress, and she even says, "It doesn't have to be like this" just as something snaps and she gasps, something is broken and again he can speak and does speak and says, "It does it does it does."

There's someone waiting for Ben when he steps out of his apartment building. A black car idling, a man holding open the back door. The driver is wearing a dark suit and black glasses and says nothing as Ben gets in. From the backseat, he watches the city pass outside his rain-washed window. Great trees shining ultra-green in the storm. Umbrellas on the rivering sidewalk. As removed from the desert as you can get. Yet still, just bodies. On the street and in every room. Bodies on top of bodies. From his jacket's inside pocket—he changed his clothes while at home, shaved and washed and now wears a black suit—Ben takes out the envelope of negatives. Looks at the inverted faces. Backward teeth and backward eyes. Did he ever know these people? Like the monochromes and sepias in his Gideon Index. Did he always know? He puts the negatives back in their paper sleeve. Sleepwalking or asleep? He tucks the envelope back into his pocket. Awake. Always awake.

The room fades to a halo of white slowly dimming to black. The darkness dissolves and becomes this room and El's given up struggling beneath him, one arm twisted all wrong under her body, her face and eyes turned away. But one hand still touches his neck. Her legs move slightly against his.

"Ben?" Her breath is a whisper in the roar of the storm. "Ben, I'm hurt."

"I know."

His words are his words again.

"I know."

The storm-light and shadow are his.

"Now please be quiet."

Wipers swishing aside the rain, the black car glides past the university and up a wooded hillside overlooking the city. Maples and birch trees, viridescent dripping wet. Am I leading with my head or with my heart? The car pulls to a stop outside a tall building, granite and brick wound tight in vines, wrought iron in the windows. Leading with my bones or leading with my blood? The driver opens Ben's door and holds an umbrella for him, guides him away from the rain-washed front steps and around the side of the building, to a short flight of stairs down to a basement door. There's a familiar crest on the bricks above the doorway. I am leading with my shadow. The driver stands aside but goes no further. Ben has to open the door himself.

Now and then, he catches passing whispers. The mention of calling security. Ben sits up and stands, walks a slow circle around the bench and the planter with its spray of banana leaves, pretends to look around. Sits again on the bench and lies down. Shuts his eyes.

To leave means distance—standing, seeing—enough to see what he's done. So he closes his eyes when he removes himself from her. The cling of her body. The cling of her smell. He closes his eyes as he removes himself from her. But even still, he can't help but see her one limp and twisted arm, crooked under her body and so obviously broken.

And the way she says his name is something lost and fleeting and already gone. She says his name like a broken prayer, and the name she prays to is no longer his name.

Outside, the storm is not abating. A wailing, lashing grey. He's certain: it never will. He cannot look back as he leaves El behind. The mask slips off as he steps through the open door. Disassembles in the premature night. His face a wet clenched fist against the wind and like a stray dog, his shadow follows him into the storm.

The corridor he enters is long and dark. The dusty smell of a library. A lit room at the hallway's end. Ben turns to see the driver standing outside the door, still at the top of the steps, but really, all Ben can see are his legs, suspended in dim light. Turning back toward the room, he hears the sound of a voice echoing toward him. Spoken by someone he cannot see. Sleepwalking or awake? Sleepwalking. Awake. Carefully on his twisted foot, Ben heads toward the room at the hallway's end. But really, he barely feels a thing.

And he can see himself so clearly now, a man walking a dark passage between two points of light. Standing in a doorway with a storm at his back. Framed in darkness and framed in light.

If there exists a mask of perfect evil, he thinks, one that poisons children and the wombs of women, is there a corresponding mask of perfect good? And as soon as he thinks this, he knows: El would know. He wishes he could have understood that sooner.

In the room's sterile light, a long burnt oak table stretches, surrounded by men with white hair and dark suits, assembled and waiting. Ben can see the pictures he gave to El spread out over the table's polished face: recoiling figures and crying eyes, everything he remembers and everything he forgot. The men lean over the pictures, hovering, tapping at them, as if proving a point. All his evidence laid out before them, and the way the corners of his mouth keep pulling, keep stretching, Ben feels his stitches widen and tear apart. He will bleed through his speech. There will always be blood in his mouth. Crossing the room, meeting eyes with no one, he takes the podium at the table's head—or is it its foot?—and nods once to everyone gathered around.

When he was a boy, Ben dreamed he was his creator's creator. When he was boy, he let the sun decide what he could and couldn't be.

"Gentlemen."

Sleepwalking or awake.

"Thank you for inviting me home."

An unseen voice echoing all around. Ben hears himself speaking, feels the blood already in his mouth.

"We're here today because of proof," and he falters, hands and breath unsteady.

And surrounding him, hungry-eyed: he sees the men lean in.

To
SLEEP
as
ANIMALS

DOUGLAS W. MILLIKEN is doing his best to stay awake, because the film is good and it's not yet dark outside. But this couch is a softly closing palm, and weeks pass between each whisper of dialogue amid these shifting desert scenes. The town lies empty and wind dances with the dust. Charles Bronson reaches for his holster, but it's a harmonica that he draws. His shadow draws faster and blows him away. Horses bray and twitch their withers as all the children clap and sing. Can't you hear them clap and sing? Douglas sways and claps and sings. But the room is empty and the light's turned low. He kicks his itchy foot with an itchy foot in the dark while the last harmonica notes tremble and fade, the shadow—victorious—steals a horse, rides away, and like far off thunder glowering in the mountains, framed in darkness and framed in light: he's awake.

MAFIC